Summer of the Skunks

summer of the skunks

Wilmoth Foreman

FRONT STREET
Asheville, North Carolina

First edition

LIBRARY OF CONGRESS CATALOGING-IN-PUBLICATION DATA

Foreman, Wilmoth
Summer of the skunks / Wilmoth Foreman.—1st ed.
p. cm.
Summary: Tells the story of ten-year-old Jill,
her brothers, sister, and parents and their life
on a southern farm in the late 1940s.
ISBN 1-886910-80-4
[1. Country life—Southern States—Fiction.
2. Family life—Southern States—Fiction.
3. Southern States—History—20th century—Fiction.]
I. Title

PZ7.F7584Su2003
[Fic]dc   2002192747

*Although the people and events in this
story are fictitious, the setting is real.
Or as real as memory can make it.*

*It is to that place—five acres with garden,
orchard, pasture, animals, and us—and to
the setting's moment in time—a good era
to grow in—that I dedicate this book.*

—W.F.

The Skunks Move In

"WAKE UP, JILL!" MAMA'S VOICE COMES SOFT BUT URGENT through my thick fog of sleep. "We've got skunks under the house."

"Uunnh?" I groan and stretch. My elbow bumps the wall.

"Shhh! No noise." Her hand is on my shoulder, calming me. "A mama skunk and her little ones. They've moved in under our house."

"How do you know?" I sniff the air. There's a faint odor of skunk, but it's no worse than if one had ambled past my window.

"Calvin saw them on his way back from milking."

I roll over to face the wall. "Guess he'll find a way to blame me for the skunks," I mutter. Lately, if he gets a hangnail, Calvin can prove it's my fault. Mama claims it's because he's at an awkward age—about to be fourteen.

She starts tiptoeing toward my door.

"Where under the house?" I ask just loud enough for her to hear.

"Probably the music room. The smell's strongest there, but they crawled in where a circulation plank's down."

I sit up so fast, the bedsprings creak. "Be quiet!" Mama shushes me. "If we scare that mama skunk, she'll spray, and this house will stink to high heavens."

What Mama doesn't know is, I'm in trouble, and I'm not even out of bed yet. Calvin will be right if he blames me for the skunks. Where our house is low to the ground, Daddy dug a trench to let air get underneath. He propped what he calls circulation planks—boards with lots of holes drilled in them—over the trench to keep animals out. A couple of days ago, while I was babysitting him, Josh started bouncing a ball off those planks. He's the one who knocked a plank down. I'm the one who should've propped it back up.

I slip one foot and then the other onto the floor, ease across the room, and hold my breath until the underwear drawer opens without sticking. Then I tiptoe to where yesterday's cutoffs are lying on the floor.

Our stairs are on the other side of my wall. As I dress, I hear Mama tip-tipping up them, probably to tell Margo. She's being so careful, the fifth step doesn't squeak.

By the time I get to breakfast, all I can smell is sausage. Everybody else is already at the table, still and quiet, like on the morning after we buried Gramps. Josh is sitting up stiff as a board, holding both hands over his mouth, big-eyed with trying not to talk. I settle into my chair next to him.

Daddy spells it out for us. "Walk in sock feet," he says. "Keep your voices down. No loud noises."

Joshua giggles. I get him in a headlock and clamp my hand over his mouth. He crosses his eyes and gouges my ribs with his elbow. I giggle, too.

"Settle down, both of you!" Daddy says loud enough that we come to attention. "Be careful how you close doors," he says to us all, then looks at Margo. "And no practicing in the house."

"But I have to practice!" Margo wails. "I have a challenge!"

Margo just finished tenth grade, and she's already first-chair French horn. Whoever's second keeps trying to beat her but hasn't won a challenge yet. She and Calvin go to band practice all summer long.

"Take your horn to the chicken house," Daddy tells her. "It's far enough away …"

"It stinks!" Margo whines. "And chickens are in there!"

"One high note and they'll leave," I say. Margo looks so pitiful, I'm sorry I said it. She'll probably never take me to the movies again.

Daddy inches his chair back without making a single scraping noise. He waits for Calvin to look up from eating, then says, "If anything upsets that mama skunk, everything in this house will stink for months."

Margo lets out a whimper. Josh starts making gagging noises.

"Who's gonna keep Josh quiet?" I ask.

"I'll call your aunt Cora," Mama says. "If Cora can't keep him"—she reaches over and tousles Josh's hair—"I guess we'll have to gag him."

"Or knock him out," Calvin mumbles.

"I'll do it!" I say it too loud. Everybody shushes me.

"How we gonna get those skunks out?" Calvin asks.

"I'll come up with something," Daddy says. "But with two men out sick at the plant, this overtime …"

Mama puts her hand over his. "We'll manage, Cliff."

Daddy gets up, stands so tall the kitchen gets smaller. "Just keep it quiet around here." He starts to leave, but adds, "One other thing. Something's knocked down one of the circulation planks. That's where the skunks got in."

Josh gets double still. So do I.

Daddy says, "Leave that plank down so the mama skunk can get out to look for food."

With Josh at Cora's, it's like I've been handed a surprise vacation from watching him. I settle in my room with a 500-piece jigsaw puzzle of look-alike puppies. I've had it a long time but haven't worked it because Josh would manage to lose some of the pieces.

The skunk smell is not bad but not good. Nobody is practicing or laughing or fussing or rattling stuff in the kitchen or clunking around in their rooms. Being surrounded by no noise gives me the willies.

The phone rings. In the quietness it sounds like a four-alarm fire. I run to catch it, and turn the ringer down as low as it'll go.

"Hey, Squirt!" It's Calvin's pal Luther, who lives up the road. "Where's Calvin?" he asks in his man-sounding voice.

I tell him Mama's got Calvin cleaning the barn today.

"Let him know I'll pick him up about four o'clock to go fishing." Luther just turned sixteen and has his driver's license.

"Hey, Luther," I say in my sweetest voice. "Would you be going to Norton's to fish?"

"You got it."

"Can I go, too?"

"That's between you and Calvin, Squirt."

Squirt. That's Luther's name for me. I like it, coming from him.

I stick a *Tom and Jerry* comic book in my back pocket and go looking for Calvin. He's in the holding pen beside our barn, digging worms. His old dog Bo is lying up against the barn, asleep in the sun. I slide through the gate and stand over Calvin. "Going to Norton's Pond?" I ask.

He keeps digging.

"I could rig up that pole you gave me in no time."

Calvin latches onto a granddaddy worm. He drops it into a tin can of dirt. It thrashes a few times, then burrows down.

"I could be ready 'fore you can say Jack Robinson." I grab a worm that's getting away and put it in the can.

"I got no need to say Jack Robinson." Calvin's voice is back and forth squeaky-croaky. With his trowel, he packs down the dirt where he dug. If he was to leave a hole, our cow Josephine might step in it and turn her ankle. He digs in a new place and mumbles, "Luther's going with me."

"Remember when I caught that big catfish last year?" I say. "Luther called me the fishingest girl he ever saw. You told him you taught me to fish when I was knee-high to a grasshopper!" I work hard to keep the whine out of my voice. "Remember telling him that, Calvin?"

Calvin keeps his head ducked. I hold my breath with hoping. Sudden and jerky, he picks up a dirt clump that's got worm ends coming out every which way. He crumbles the dirt, worms and all, into the can, levels off the dug place, and stands up.

"Can I go?" I beg. "Luther likes me. He won't care."

"Nope." Calvin puts his worms in the shade and starts shoveling manure into the wheelbarrow.

"Luther won't care." My voice sounds about to cry. "Why'd you give me a pole if I can't go fishing?"

Calvin scrapes up a shovelful of manure too close to my shoe and says, "Your pole is welcome to go with us."

"Luther'll be here about four." I say it real hateful, stomp out of the holding pen, and plop down on the feed room step to read. Maybe I'll beg again in a few minutes.

Barney, the mama cat that births all her litters in the feed room, rubs against my back a few times, then wanders off. A kitten runs after her. Barney growls, rears up on her haunches, and slaps the kitten fast with both front paws. It backs off and Barney goes about her business alone.

Calvin comes by, headed to the garden. He sets the over-loaded wheelbarrow down and stares straight ahead. "Jill."

I turn a page I haven't even finished and pretend I'm reading.

"Jill! I've still got most of the pen to shovel out."

"So?"

"Will you help?"

"Why?"

"I can't finish it alone before Luther gets here."

"So?"

He studies on that. "If you'll help, I'll loan you my Monopoly set."

"I got nobody to play it with." I let that sink in. "I'd rather go fishing." I grin up at him. "With you and Luther."

He gives me a "you're disgusting" look. "Not today. Maybe next week."

I pick at a scab on my elbow. He hates that. "No later than next Tuesday." I flick the scab near his boot. "And say please."

Without the please, Calvin trots off with the wheelbarrow, leaving a trail of manure clumps that fall overboard. Bo gets up, scratches his ear with his hind foot, and ambles off after Calvin.

I stare after them. This time last summer, I was right there with Bo, tagging along after Calvin. We were all the time doing stuff. Like fixing up this little cave we found in a hill in our pasture. We built shelves along the cave's back wall. One for his arrowheads, one for my rock collection.

I can picture Calvin now, squatted on his heels arranging arrowheads and eating potato chips. He eats all the time. "This'll be our place, Jill-girl," he said. He handed me a curled chip, my favorite kind. "Nobody else can come here. Just us."

This summer, Calvin gets mad if I even mention the cave. Last week I told him, "I found a new arrowhead. It's on your shelf in our cave." He looked at me like I was speaking in some foreign language, then walked away.

The kitten that Barney swatted comes rubbing around my ankles. I pick it up, smooth its gray fur, and hug on it. "I know how you feel," I say in its ear. It starts purring up a storm.

Calvin comes trotting down the path with our other flat shovel rattling in the wheelbarrow. I dump the kitten out of my lap and bury my head in the comic book. He stops in front of me and says, "Got you a shovel."

"You never said please, Calvin."

He leans my shovel against the barn and heads for the holding pen. I take the shovel and follow him.

The manure is bone dry and doesn't have much smell. We've got the job half finished before Calvin says, in his "pals" voice, "I've got a plan, Jill."

"What kind of plan?" I try to sound so-so, but my heart starts pounding.

"That's for me to know and you to find out," this-summer's Calvin says. He grabs the wheelbarrow and heads for the garden. But when he gets back with the empty barrow, he says, "A plan to get the skunks out."

I start shoveling fast. I don't want to act too interested.

"Me and you and Margo could do it," he says.

Me and them. Me. And them. I like the sound of that. I don't care what the plan is.

"What about Daddy?" I can't help but ask. "He said he'd think of something."

"Two men on his shift are out bad sick. It could be days—maybe weeks—before Daddy's home long enough to do anything but eat and sleep." Calvin leans on his shovel. He gets that "confidential" look he used to get when he'd tell me one of his plans. "I've thought up a way we can get those skunks out and save Daddy a lot of worry." He slides his shovel under a clump of manure.

I shovel hard to keep from grinning. Last year's Calvin is back. Planning and figuring. Telling *me*. "How we gonna scare the skunks out?" I ask.

"Not scare 'em, dopey. Move 'em."

Mama's "Come here, Jill" whistle sounds loud and clear from the backyard. She's got a different whistle for each of us. Even Josh.

Calvin winks at me. "Don't say nothing yet." He moves the wheelbarrow closer to what's left of the manure. "It's our secret, Jill-girl."

I prop my shovel against the barn and head for the house. In my mind I sing over and over, "Calvin needs me to help with the skunks, Calvin needs me to help with the skunks."

Once I'm out of Calvin's sight, I can't help skipping in time to the song in my head.

Mama is in the swing. I skip right past her.

"Jill." She pats a spot for me to sit beside her. "I need your help."

She starts in before I get settled, "If Margo isn't ready for that challenge she could lose her first-place chair." Mama gives a little sigh. "She's real upset about it. Help me think of a place she can practice."

I'm a good thinker, so I say right off, "She could go to Clare's."

"That would work," Mama says, "if there were a way to get her there."

I almost say, "Luther could take her," but Mama's not too happy about Calvin riding with Luther. She sure wouldn't let precious Margo set foot in a car he's driving.

We swing awhile with no talking. Whenever Mama's foot nudges the ground to keep us moving, the swing creaks. I'm glad the skunks can't hear it.

"Margo could practice in the feed room," I say. "It's a pretty clean place."

"Margo's not used to the barn," Mama says.

She's right about that. When we moved out here, Margo was about the age I am now. I've heard time and again about how she pitched a fit over leaving her friends in town. The first time she saw this place, she swore, "I'll never set foot outside the mowed yard!"

Margo hasn't exactly kept that promise. She goes with us when Mama fixes a picnic in the pasture. And when Josie has a new calf or Barney has kittens, Margo goes to the barn to see them. A couple of years ago, she was so taken with a fluffy yellow kitten, she brought him to the house, bottle-fed and tamed him, and named him Butterball. Before Butterball was full grown, he got killed by a stray dog.

Margo still goes back to look every time Barney has new kittens. But she doesn't love on them. And she doesn't keep visiting them like me and Calvin and Josh do.

"Would you stay at the feed room with Margo?" Mama asks.

I like the sound of that. Me watching over Margo, who never wants me within miles of her.

"I guess I'll go." I say it like I wish I didn't have to. "But you ask her. You know she won't try it if I ask."

In no time Margo comes out the back door with her horn case and a folded music stand. She calls over her shoulder to Mama, "I'm coming right back if I don't like it."

I lead the way. Calvin comes charging down the path toward us with a wheelbarrow of manure. He acts like we aren't even there. When we step aside to let him and Bo pass, Margo brushes up against some stick-tights.

"Shewee!" Margo holds her nose. "That manure stinks."

"It's supposed to," I say. I don't tell her how much worse it could be if it was fresh or wet.

"I'm not staying if the feed room smells like that!" she says.

"It smells like feed." I help pick stick-tights off her

slacks. "A good, sweet smell. You should've worn something slouchy."

"I don't own anything slouchy. If I did, I'd throw it away."

I carry the horn so Margo can watch out for stick-tights. Josephine is in the barnyard, cropping grass along the far fence. If I know Calvin, he's on his way to the house for a snack. It looks like Margo and I are on our own. I hope Josie's in a good mood.

At the gate, I set the horn down and tell Margo, "Wait here till I get the feed room door open."

"Is Josephine gonna chase me?" she asks.

"Probably not, unless you run. Walk real regular. Sudden moves make her nervous."

"I wish I hadn't come back here." Margo's voice is getting louder and shriller with every word. "I'm scared of cows, and—"

"You're gonna hurt Josephine's feelings," I warn her. I open the gate, show Margo how to fasten it behind her, say "I'll signal you," and amble the short distance to the barn.

Josie slow-motions her neck in my direction and flicks her tail at a horsefly that's settled on her haunches. She greets me with a soft low. This may be one of her good days.

I inch the feed room door open. Barney's half-wild kittens scatter in all directions. The little gray one starts to run but stops and peeks out from behind a feed sack. Barney saunters over for me to scratch her head, then hops down the step and wanders off toward the fencerow.

I signal Margo, but she just stands there looking miserable.

"Come on!" I mouth the words.

Margo scoots her horn through the gate, creeps through, and fiddles with the latch. Josephine is watching her. Strands of grass hang from Josie's mouth, wobbling as she chews.

"She's looking at me!" Margo wails in a high trembly voice.

"It's okay," I say real quiet. "Just walk slow and don't act afraid."

Margo doesn't budge until Josephine reaches down for more grass. Then she grabs her horn and starts running.

"Slow down!" I say it strong enough that she slows.

About six feet from the door Margo screams, "Snake! Snake!" She drops the horn, bolts like a spooked horse, and nearly knocks me down as she clambers up the feed room step. She's shaking and clutching at me and pointing at the path where the horn is. "Snake!" she screams again.

"Shut up, Margo! It's just a black racer," I tell her. Josie lets out an urgent, high-pitched grunt and lowers her head. "Now look what you've done!"

Josie trots toward us, lifting her hooves high like a show horse and snuffling under her breath. The whites of her eyes are showing; her tail is hiked up.

"My horn!" Margo wails. Josie hooks at the case, but her horns are curved toward each other, so they just bounce the case around without stabbing it. "Get my horn, Jill!" Margo begs.

Josie butts the horn closer to the barn. Margo grabs my shoulder and starts shaking me. "It belongs to the school. We'll never get it paid off." She yells toward the house, "Calvin!"

"Will you shut up?" I say through clenched teeth. "I'll get your precious horn."

By now, Josie seems more curious than mad. She nuzzles the case and taps it again with her horns. I scoop some feed into a bucket and ease down the steps.

"Keep the door clear," I tell Margo. I creep near enough for Josie to smell the feed, then put down the bucket, crooning, "Atta girl. Come and get it, Josie."

Josephine sniffs the bucket. I grab the horn case, run for the feed room, and scramble up the steps. When I look back, Josie is eating calm as you please.

Margo reaches for the case and then draws back. "It's got cow slobber on it!" she moans. She won't touch the case until I wipe it off with an empty sack.

We fix a feed sack chair and set up the music stand. "You'd better start out soft," I tell her, "to get Josie used to listening. And you might want to thank the person who saved you and your French horn from a cow."

Without a word, Margo flattens her lips to fit the mouthpiece and puts her hand in the horn's bell to muffle the sound.

It's me that can't stand being cooped up in that little room with muffled scales squeezing their way out of a French horn. I go out and sit on the step to read. I'm in chapter three of *Little House on the Prairie* and Calvin's still not back when Margo calls out, "Oh, Jill? Could you come here a minute?"

She's ready to leave. She closes the horn case and says, "That wasn't so awful." She digs a tube of lipstick out of her pocket and slathers it on. Like me or Josephine give a hoot what she looks like. Anyway, Josie has wandered into the pasture out of sight.

Margo smiles her Miss Perfect Teeth smile. "How do I look, Jill?"

She stands straight and flounces her hair all around her face. The sun coming through the feed room door has her in its spotlight. Her eyes are green today, my favorite of the colors they change to. They're flirting with me, asking for the right answer.

"You look like a beauty queen," I say.

The smile turns real. "Thanks. Do you mean it?"

I curve my elbow out like an usher did for me at Cousin Betsy's wedding. "May I escort Miss Feed Room to the gate?"

"What about my horn?"

"Beauty queens don't tote French horns. I'll come back for it."

We walk off, arm in arm, toward a house with skunks under it. But we wouldn't be arm in arm if it wasn't for those skunks.

Luther shows up. I help load his car with fishing poles, a stringer, nets. Maybe Calvin will forget that my payback fishing trip is not supposed to be today.

I stand real close to the back seat door when Luther and Calvin are about to leave. Luther starts the engine. "See ya, Squirt," he says. Calvin doesn't say anything. He picks up the can of worms, gets in the front, and slams his door.

Me and Bo watch until Luther's car disappears around the far curve. Because of helping Calvin, I'm behind on my own chores. I fold the clean clothes and put them away, then set the table for supper. We eat without Calvin. Mama fixes a plate for him and leaves it on the stove.

It's after dark when Calvin gets home. I pour him a tall glass of cold buttermilk, then watch him eat. He hunkers down over his plate, shovels in mashed potatoes, beans, raw onion, and cornbread, and gulps big swigs of buttermilk.

I say, "Guess who saved Margo from a snake and a cow today?"

Calvin picks up his pork chop and gnaws down to the bone. "Bo?" he asks through a mouthful of meat. He stands up mid-chew, leaves his supper dishes for me to clean up without even asking, and heads out to dress the fish.

There's a table under our backyard floodlight for jobs too messy for the kitchen, like cleaning fish. I wander out there, in case Calvin wants to tell me his skunk plan.

He grips a catfish by its head and slits the skin along the back edge of its head bone. With pliers, he grabs the skin and pulls it all the way down to the tail. It sounds like paper being ripped out of some huge, slippery notebook. He throws the strip of skin into a bucket of water that's on the ground beside him. It splashes on me.

"Get out of the way," he says without looking up.

I stomp to the house and go to bed not knowing the skunk plan. But whatever it is, Calvin and I have a secret.

Because of the skunks, Josh is at Cora's again. Mama's busy sewing and doesn't think to give me any jobs. By mid-afternoon, doing whatever I want gets tiresome. I wander into the kitchen.

Margo has set up her manicure stuff on the kitchen table, since Josh isn't here to get into it. I watch the whole time she does her nails, but she acts like I'm not there. While the last coat dries, she goes to the living room to talk on the phone.

I borrow a bottle of her polish. The more I paint, the gunkier my nails look. Margo starts rustling around like she's off the phone. I hurry to get the top on the polish without smearing my nails worse than they already are.

Margo comes into the kitchen, takes one look, and swells up ready to yell. I point toward the music room and say, "Skunks, Margo."

"Pest!" she whisper-hisses in my face. She grabs my wrists and holds them tight to look at my messy nails. "Meddlesome pesky brat!" She's so mad, it's all she can do to whisper.

Real quiet, I remind her again, "Don't scare our skunks."

A calmness wraps around Margo like the chocolate coating on a Dairy Queen cone. But her anger is frozen underneath. She sloshes polish remover on a wad of cotton balls and motions for me to sit. Fast and furious, she rubs my left thumbnail clean.

The minute the last nail is plain and looks like it belongs to me again, I get up to leave. But Margo motions me back into the chair. She cleans under my nails, trims and files them, and then starts polishing. Without a word she shows me how to stay away from the edges so the polish won't fuzz up.

The first coat takes forever to dry. "I'm tired of setting here," I whine.

"You're not a hen," Margo snaps. "Unless there's a nest of eggs under you, you're *sitting*, not *setting*." She touches the first nail she polished and starts on its second coat. "S-I-T still," she spells. I breathe shallow so as not to move my hands or choke on the sharp polish smell. Margo finishes two coats of red and one clear, then looks steady into my eyes. She smiles her beauty-pageant smile and says, "Get lost."

I lock myself in the bathroom and let the faucet trickle

to sound like I'm brushing my teeth or washing up. I breathe a film on the mirror. With my painted fingernails I make fluttery, fancy-lady motions. The blur of my red nails through the breath-film looks like colors in a floating dream. I write "Jill" in the film, check to be sure the door is locked, and write "Luther."

There's this quiet knock on the door. It may have been going on awhile, mixed in with the running water sound. I turn off the faucet.

"Jill." Calvin must have his mouth right on the crack in the door. "Jill, can you hear me?"

I tiptoe to put my mouth near where I think his is. "Yesssss," I whisper.

"How long you gonna be? I need in there, *bad*."

"I'm about out." I flush the commode and wipe the mirror with a used towel before unlocking the door. So far, the mama skunk doesn't mind hearing the toilet flush.

"Thanks, Jill-girl," Calvin whispers.

If this had been a day without skunks, Calvin would have hollered and about pounded the door down. And Margo would've mossed over before she'd have painted a single one of my nails.

I settle down in my room to read. Without knocking, Margo tiptoes in. She goes to the bureau and picks up her brush—she has brushes all over the place—and combs her fingers through her hair. She starts brushing, watching herself in the big mirror above my bureau. I stare.

Margo notices me cross-legged on the bed, holding a book but watching her. In a loud whisper she asks, "Whatcha reading?"

"Nothing right now," I whisper back. "I'm watching you. Brush your hair. In my room."

"I'm in a hurry," she whispers. "Calvin and I are going to town."

"So?"

It's hard to sound nasty whispering to somebody who's clear across the room. I get a straight chair and set it next to the dresser so I can lean on my elbows and stare up at her.

Margo bends over and starts brushing her hair upside down, away from her head. "Really, Jill. Whatcha reading?"

"*Black Beauty.*"

"Twenty-six, twenty-seven …" she counts. At forty, she says, "*Black Beauty*? That's about a horse, isn't it?"

"Yes."

"A horse!" She hears how loud she's said it and goes back to a whisper. "Why read about a horse?"

"Because …" The answer isn't in me. "I like it. This is the fifth time I've read it."

She stops brushing and turns so she can peer at me from under the curtain of black hair. "You need a library card." She flips her hair over her head and starts brushing it straight back. "Fifty-one, fifty-two …"

"I have a library card. You know that."

"Then use it."

"Why are you all the time brushing?"

I've forgotten to sound hateful. But so has Margo. At eighty-eight, she asks, "Is my hair shiny?"

"Yes."

She keeps brushing, like she's studying her answer. "Ninety-nine, one hundred." She looks at me in the mirror. "How do they get horses' coats to shine?"

"They curry 'em."

"With ... ?"

"With a curry brush, of course."

Margo waves her brush in my face, then lays it on the bureau. She points to her hair and says, "Shiny." She points to the brush, whispers, "Brush," and taps my forehead where my brain is. "Got it, Jill?" She pats me on the head and leaves.

I start to holler, "Can I go with you and Calvin?" but then I remember the skunks.

There's no point in running to ask. The answer's gonna be no.

My nails are the only bright spots in this morning. Black clouds are rolling in, and thunder rumbles in the distance. The thick, stormy air makes the skunk smell so much worse, today's sausage can't drown it out.

A furnace broke down at the plant, and Daddy's shorthanded crew has to fix it. He left before breakfast. Josh spent the night at Cora's.

The lightning is getting closer, so I go to the kitchen. Mama and Calvin and Margo are already there. Margo is at the table, marking things in the Sears, Roebuck catalog. Once she finishes picking out socks, underwear, material to sew for school clothes, maybe a sweater, I get to mark what I want.

I use a green pencil. Margo can't stand for me to copy her, so I can't mark anything she's circled in pink. But I always wish I could.

When it's my turn with the catalog, once I pick out school clothes, I'm gonna circle a few hope-fors. Like Sears' best jump rope. And a ball glove. I've never had a glove except Calvin's worn-out ones. As much overtime as

Daddy's putting in, it can't hurt to try.

The storm's getting closer. Calvin finds our flashlights while Mama rummages through a cabinet for candles, in case the electricity goes out.

A loud crash makes us all jump. The lights splutter and die. Layer after layer of thunder rolls over our roof.

"Sounds like lightning hit a transformer," Mama says. "We may be without lights till nighttime."

What with the black clouds and the shade of the catalpa tree outside the kitchen door, it's almost as dark as night.

"Is this gonna scare our skunks?" Margo asks. She's holding a flashlight for Mama. I ease into a chair across the table from Calvin.

"Probably not." Mama dribbles hot candle wax into a jar top, sticks the candle in the wax, and sets it on the table. "That mama skunk's glad she's not getting rained on." Mama takes the flashlight and heads off toward the bathroom.

Margo sinks into a chair and lays her head on her arms. "I'm sick of this," she whispers. "We could start back to school smelling like skunk."

Her hair is so close to the candle, Calvin moves it. He catches my eye and mouths, "My Plan."

"We could get the skunks out," he says in a whisper-croak. "The three of us."

Margo sits up and looks at him real hard. I let "the three of us" sound again and again in my head. Calvin turns the candle's jar top round and round. He always fiddles with something when he talks serious. "I thought about it the whole time I cleaned the barn," he says. "And while I mowed."

"Here comes Mama," I say. We quit whispering.

Lightning hits something down the road and I about jump out of my skin.

"Sissy scaredy-pants," Calvin sneers.

"Don't start that," Mama says. She relays her flashlight to Margo, who heads for the bathroom.

Calvin's never gonna tell his plan with Mama in the room. As soon as her back is turned, I point at her and ask him real innocent-like, "Why don't you get the Monopoly?" Mama hates to play Monopoly.

Calvin catches on. He winks at me. "Oh, all right." He says it grumbly so Mama will think everything's normal. He takes a flashlight with him upstairs, comes back with the game, and starts setting it up. "Hey, Mama! Wanna play Monopoly?" he asks.

She picks up a candle and matches. "Think I'd rather pay bills by candlelight." She reaches for the flashlight Margo has brought back. On her way to the living room table where she does our bookkeeping, Mama warns us, "If there's one argument, even a quiet one, this game is over."

That's my ticket to stay in the game. If Calvin or Margo tries to leave me out, I'm gonna argue up a storm. A worse storm than the one that got our lights.

Calvin leans in close as he doles out the money. "We can lure that mama skunk out"—because he's trying to talk quiet, his voice goes up and down worse than ever—"then close the gap in the planks and go in after the babies."

"Can I be banker?" I whisper.

"No! Shut up and listen!" Calvin glances toward the living room, flings my hundreds at me, and tries to whisper. "Margo?" He clears his throat. "You know that little trap door where Daddy goes under the house to fix the pipes?"

He looks at her real serious. "You can crawl under there to get the skunk babies."

Margo aims her worst glare at Calvin, but he keeps on. "I know you could crawl if you set your mind to it."

Margo gives a little ladylike snort. "I'd move to the barn before I'd crawl under the house."

"It might save you and your stuff from smelling like skunks ..."

She raises her eyebrows and starts arranging her money under the edge of the Monopoly board. "Jill's little. Let her do the crawling."

Calvin frowns. "You know she won't get it right."

"Will, too!" I come back at him. He acts like he didn't hear. I think fast and add, "Besides, I know under the house like the back of my hand."

They both gawk at me. To cancel the lie, I put my hands in my lap and cross my fingers. "I was just under there—again—a few days ago." I cross my toes and begin to arrange my money. "I sure would like to be banker."

"Let her be banker," Margo says. "I'll take over if she messes up."

Calvin has looked skunks up in the encyclopedia. "They sleep in daytime," he says, "and look for food at night." He leans over the board and motions for us to listen close. "We'll lay a trail of apple bits to lure the mama out to the barnyard. Margo, you'll watch from your window upstairs. When that mama skunk comes out from under the house and starts following the apple trail, all you gotta do is signal me with three blinks of the flashlight. I'll signal Jill to crawl under."

"I can do that," Margo says.

"The minute the skunk's out of sight, Margo, you run

down and fix the plank so she can't get back under the house. Jill will hand the babies out to me."

Something dawns on me. "Those little skunks are gonna spray me when I try to catch them!"

Calvin gives me his "Don't you know anything?" look. "Skunks can't spray till they're pretty good size, dummy." He sounds so close to arguing, I look in Mama's direction.

"The *Farmers' Almanac* says tonight's a full moon," Calvin whispers. "We can see to do it."

"What if Josh is here?" I ask. "What if it's still storming?"

"Think, Jill." Calvin rolls his eyes at Margo. "Josh goes to bed before dark and sleeps like a log. If it's raining, we wait till tomorrow night."

By afternoon the storm is gone, so we hide flashlights, apples, and a paring knife outside. Margo is about to cry. "I am not a sneaky person," she says.

"You either help or breathe skunk till Daddy's overtime lightens up," Calvin reminds her.

We go to bed like any other night. Without meaning to, I go to sleep. Margo touches my shoulder. "It's time," she whispers. I sit bolt upright, wide awake, hoping the skunks didn't hear my bedsprings.

At the crawl space door, the moonlight is spooky. There's barely enough for me to see Calvin hurry down the barn path. When he climbs the lookout apple tree, he looks like his own shadow.

Waiting stretches into forever. Bo is whining soft and mournful in the garage. Calvin keeps him in there at night and sometimes in daytime when he doesn't want a dog trailing his every step.

I look around till I find a long, stout stick to take under the house, in case something mean is hiding under there. Then I sit on a rock where I can see Calvin's tree.

Bo's whining gets louder. The mama skunk must be going past the garage. The apple-trail part of Calvin's plan is working!

Bo hardly ever barks, but I cross my fingers to keep him from it now. When the skunks are gone, it's gonna be so good to make noise again. I can yell at Josh. And stomp my foot when Margo fusses at me.

But Calvin will go back to yelling at me. And it'll be my job again to babysit Josh nonstop. And Margo will be slamming doors. On second thought, I may *miss* having skunks under the house.

Calvin blinks his flashlight three times—my cue that the mama skunk has passed the apple tree.

I open the trap door, count to a hundred, take a deep breath, and crawl under.

Moon or no moon, under the house is dark. All Calvin gave me is a penlight. I angle it toward the music room corner where the indoor smell is strongest.

The darkness is like some solid thing closing in around me. Looking at it makes me breathe harder. And worry more. Something as silly as a slug on that circulation plank could send Margo into a tizzy fit. If she doesn't fix the plank good enough to keep the mama out, I could get stuck under here with a grownup skunk.

By stretching my foot backwards, I can still touch the trap door. "Sissy scaredy-pants," Calvin hisses in my mind's ear. I quit thinking and crawl into the thick darkness. The cool feel of the packed dirt floor against my bare arms and legs gives me the shivers.

"Is that you bleeding, or the skunk?" Calvin asks.

I touch the ponk-knot. But it's my arm that's bloody. I wipe it on my shorts. Two jagged breaks in my skin ooze more blood.

"Aw, Jill-girl." Calvin lays the shirtful of skunk on the ground and holds it with his foot. He examines my arm. "Can't tell if it's a bite or a scratch." He reaches over to wipe my hair away from the knot on my forehead. "You're liable to have to take rabies shots."

He picks up the shirtful of wiggling skunk and holds it at arm's length on the way to the backyard. I squeeze my arm to make the places bleed more. I've heard about shots for rabies. How people who take them have to be locked in little rooms until they get every one of their shots. How if the shots don't work, the people go mad and foam at the mouth.

I wonder, if I get locked in a room, will Margo and Calvin look in through the little window and get disgusted? Maybe Margo will blame herself, for not taking the crawler job. Maybe Calvin will put a wet washrag on the end of a stick to reach in and wipe foam off my mouth.

Margo is sitting on the ground with the first two little skunks cradled in her lap. In the dawn light, she looks like a picture I saw once of baby Jesus' mother, her head bowed over the new baby, her body filled up with the touching.

"Take this," Calvin says. He holds the skunk shirt out to Margo.

She doesn't look up. "They're so precious," she says. This same Margo wouldn't even touch Ears, my pet rabbit. Said he stunk. She finally notices the wiggly shirt. "What's that?"

"The last skunk baby," Calvin tells her. "We gotta keep it in case it has rabies."

The skunk odor isn't much stronger when I get to their corner. My penlight shines on a wad of black and white wedged back in the narrowness of an uphill slope. The ball of fur is bigger than a couple of skunk babies should make. They may be half grown. I ease my stick toward them, wishing I'd worn gloves. And maybe a gas mask.

To free up my hands, I lay my penlight so it's shining on the skunks. The minute my stick touches fur, sleepy grunts start up. I jiggle the stick. A skunk baby rolls down. When I grab it, it lets out a little squeal and starts hissing.

With both hands, I cup the little skunk to me where it can hear my heart, and rock side to side on my elbows, humming a one-note sound. Through its fur I can feel the terror shifting back to sleepiness. I snug it close and ease one hand off; it doesn't try to get away.

The other babies are grunting but still half asleep. I reach with the stick and nudge another one. It topples down the slope to where I can scoop it up.

While I settle the second one down, the one that's still loose hisses and backs toward the far corner. I can't carry three skunks at once anyway. I'll come back for the feisty one.

I angle the penlight so its feeble beam points the way to the trap door. With skunk babies cradled under my chin, I crawl with my elbows to keep from squashing them. The babies wiggle and grunt and nuzzle. Their cool, soft paw pads and damp wandering noses send whisper chills along my bare skin.

Calvin is at the trap door, shining his flashlight right in my eyes. "You got 'em?" he asks. He snaps off the light when I turn my head away.

"There's another one." I hand him the first two. "I need help catching it."

"Three?" Calvin looks at the baby skunks, rubs his thumb on one of them. "We gotta hurry," he tells me. "I'll take these to Margo." He leaves and I crawl back into the darkness.

Every time I shine my penlight on the last skunk baby, it scrunches tighter into the narrow space between the floor and the ground. The fur around its face is trembling to beat sixty.

I suck in my stomach to get flatter, and squirm closer to the skunk. It growls. "You go right ahead, sweet thing," I purr, petting it with my voice, like when I tamed the hurt rabbit.

Calvin is outside the trap door, pounding on his flashlight, fussing because it's getting dim. The skunk growls at me again. From the way it's acting, I bet it's fourteen in skunk years.

Calvin crawls in, blocking what little light is coming through the trap door. "Got that last one yet, Jill-girl?"

"Not yet!" That's twice in two days he's called me Jill-girl. Two skunk days. Now that I'm close enough to catch this last skunk baby, I'm not sure I want to.

Instead of prying the skunk toward me, I poke it with my stick and whisper, "Get lost, skunk!" It makes an exploding noise and takes off toward the farthest corner.

Calvin crawls up beside me. "You got it, Jill?" He sounds downright friendly.

"I just about had it." I mumble so the lie doesn't sound so big. "It slipped outta my hands. Just about bit me." I can't seem to stop the fibs.

"Dang! You've ruined the whole plan!" Calvin lays his forehead down on the dirt, like its coolness can calm him. "I should've talked Margo into doing the crawling." He raises up and shines his flashlight around. "Where's the damn skunk?"

"No call for you to cuss," I say. "I couldn't help it."

I aim my penlight to our right, where the skunk went. Calvin shines his flashlight in that direction and whispers loud, "Gimme the stupid stick!"

"I tried that already."

He jerks the stick out of my hand. "Margo's out there with those other two"—Calvin's voice is cracking like crazy and it's louder than it ought to be—"and the mama's probably on her way back." He crawls toward the skunk. "Damn it, Jill! We gotta catch this one!"

"Don't cuss," I say automatic. I feel clammy, cornered. I shouldn't have scared that skunk. Calvin will never let me help again. I call in his direction, "Maybe if we throw the stick back there ..."

Calvin flings the stick and hits the skunk. It squeals and takes off toward the trap door at a dead run, shooting right past me. I make a grab for it. Fur slips through my fingers but I've slowed it down. I lunge again. My head hits rafter.

"I've got it!" I yell. The skunk scratches and bites at and tries to wrap itself around my hand. I latch on to scruff of its neck. "I've got it for sure!"

I feel a ponk-knot growing on my forehead. Calvin ers past me toward the trap door. By the time I get he's outside, shedding his shirt. I hand the skunk out

"This'll calm it," he says, wrapping the shirt aro skunk. "Settle down, little hellion."

I crawl out and stand up, studying whether "h a cuss word. The sky is getting lighter. A bir sleepy wake-up song in the mock-orange bush.

Margo is dreamy-eyed. "Let's keep them all."

"Mama won't let us," Calvin says.

Margo doesn't reach for the shirtful of skunk, so I take it. I might as well. If it's got rabies, so do I.

"I'll get something to put this one in," Calvin says. "When I get back, I'll take the others and leave them where their mama can find 'em." He hustles off toward the tool-shed. When he passes the garage, Bo starts whimpering puppylike. Calvin shushes him and keeps going. Bo doesn't hush.

Margo keeps petting the skunks that are asleep in her lap. One of them twitches, but not in a scared way. The one I'm holding in the shirt rustles around now and then, but it's quieted down a lot.

I'd like to touch Margo's two skunk babies. But I might give them rabies. I wonder what foaming at the mouth tastes like.

Calvin comes back with the cats' carrying case. He unwraps the shirt and dumps the skunk into the case. It lands on its back, jumps up, and starts hissing. Calvin slams the door, then scoops up Margo's skunks and starts at a trot toward the barn.

"Oh, let me tell 'em bye!" Margo begs.

"No time," Calvin hollers over his shoulder.

Mama comes out the kitchen door, wrapping her house-coat around her. "What're you kids up to this time of morning?" she asks.

"We got the skunks out from under the house," I tell her. "Calvin's taking two of them to their mama." I point at the skunk in the case. "We're keeping this one. And I've got rabies."

—

We wait for Dr. Jessup in the parking lot at his veterinarian office. I'm in the front seat, not because I may be dying with rabies, but so Margo can be in back with the skunk baby and Calvin. Josh is up here, too. He's hanging over the seat back, kicking me every time he tries to reach the skunk cage. All things considered, the front seat isn't so great this trip.

Margo is begging to keep the skunk.

"I don't want to hear another word about it," Mama tells her. "We're here to check for rabies, and that's the end of it."

"I heard on the radio where they thought a stray dog had rabies," I say. "They cut its head off to find out."

Josh giggles. Calvin kicks the back of my seat real hard. "All we gotta do is keep this skunk penned up, dummy," he says.

I sneak a look back at Margo. She's biting her lip and looking out the window. Two big tears are running down her face. I'm pretty sure she's worried about the skunk's head, not mine.

Dr. Jessup pulls his car in next to ours. Before his door is half open, Mama's out there telling him about the skunk and me. She motions for me to come show him my arm. He turns it this way and that before he unlocks the office door. "Probably nothing to worry about," he says.

He leads us back to one of the little rooms where he gives dog and cat shots. We all crowd in while he puts on his doctor coat and some gloves. Even this early, the room has a mediciny smell that can make me woozy if I give it a chance.

Dr. Jessup sets our skunk on the examining table. It puts its nose down and makes a beeline for the edge of the table.

Dr. Jessup turns it and lets it nearly run off the table edge again and again. Then he picks the skunk up. Rubbing its fur the wrong way, he looks at its front, back, underbelly. He checks its eyes and ears. Real sudden, he prizes the little mouth open with his big, thick fingers.

The skunk tries to hiss, but it comes out more like a choking sound.

Dr. Jessup chuckles. "Don't like that much, do you, little fellow?" He snugs the skunk baby up against his white jacket and pets on it before putting it back in the case.

"This seems to be a pretty healthy specimen," he tells us. He takes what looks like cat food out of his pocket and pokes a couple of pieces through the case wire. The skunk sniffs one and gobbles them both down. "He's old enough to know how to eat." He feeds the skunk two more pellets. "We could send his head off to the lab ..."

Margo makes a worse choking sound than the skunk did. "No-o-o! Please, no," she begs.

Dr. Jessup looks at Mama. "Or you could keep him penned up for two weeks." He pats the carrying case. "If he starts acting peculiar, you'll need to let me know right away."

Margo pleads at Mama with her eyes. Mama nods yes.

Dr. Jessup chuckles and says, "Call me before you turn him loose." He starts out the door.

"Dr. Jessup!" Margo sounds urgent. "Have you ever descented a skunk?"

"Well, yes, I have." He says it before he notices Mama shaking her head no at him.

Mama gives Margo a warning look. Margo ignores her and asks, "How much does it cost?"

"It's not cheap." Dr. Jessup half closes the door and

frowns at Margo. It's like the rest of us have disappeared and it's just him and her. "The main thing is what it costs the skunk. That odor is its only protection. It can never roam wild again." He leaves without giving Margo a money price.

We take me to the people doctor next. The skunk was in line ahead of me because Dr. Jessup's office opens earlier than Dr. Thatcher's. Mama thinks I won't have to take shots. But she gets worry lines on her forehead when she looks at me.

Dr. Thatcher gives us some ointment for my wound and says, "Don't give the shots another thought." But we have to call him every two days to report on my arm and to tell him how the skunk's acting.

When we get home, we build a skunk cage. Calvin does most of the work. I help hold the lumber, and Margo bosses us.

Mama told us not to touch the skunk, on account of he may be rabid. But two or three times during the cage building, Margo lifts him out of the carrying case just to pet on him.

I can't figure her out. We've all the time got animals around this place. Regular ones like dogs and cats, and wild ones like Ears, the hurt rabbit I tamed. Ever since a dog killed her yellow kitten, Margo hasn't paid a bit of attention to any of them. Now, she's moon-eyed over this skunk baby.

I show her how to put the skunk on the ground and feed him a raisin or bread crust, then take a step or two and put down more food. That little skunk starts tagging after Margo, looking for a treat. Margo thinks he loves her. What he loves is lunch.

I'm so worn out from going to doctors, building cages, and teaching Margo to tame a skunk, I go to bed without Mama having to say a word.

A racket jolts me awake in the night. Dogs are barking—Bo's bark in the garage mixed in with others. Somebody's running loud down the stairs. Daddy's hollering. The screen door slams.

I hit the floor practically running in my sleep. Just as I get to the back door, the BB gun pop-pops and dogs start yelping. Two strays slink down the driveway, their tails between their legs. One of them is limping. Bo is still barking nonstop.

In the floodlight Daddy's long shadow sprawls halfway across the yard. I run past him to the skunk pen. Calvin and Margo are already there. Margo is wringing her hands and whimpering while Calvin fiddles with the cage front where the wire is dented.

"Will you shut up?" he says to Margo. "They didn't get him."

Mama shows up carrying a half-asleep Josh. Daddy comes over and tugs on the cage wire.

"That'll hold till morning," he says. "You young'uns go on back to bed." He tucks the BB gun under his arm. "Those two strays won't be back for a while."

"Daddy, reckon they're the same dogs that got Margo's kitten and our hen?" Calvin asks. We had a hen that kept flying out of the chicken pen. Last week I found her bones and feathers in the barnyard.

"Probably." Daddy shakes his head. "I should'a used the shotgun." He and Mama and Josh start for the house.

Margo undoes the cage door and reaches into a back

corner for the skunk. She cuddles him under her /
ting and soothing him. The skunk sets the /
Margo's pajama top to trembling. "He's sh /
leaf," she says. "Calvin, get me the carrying /

Calvin stares at her and says, "You'd bet/
we both know what Margo has in mind. /

"It'll just be for one night," Margo /
gonna get the case or do I have to?"

My room is right below Margo's. That little sk /
scratching is so loud, it sounds like he's beside my bed. It'll
be a wonder if he doesn't worry a hole in the carrying case.

Margo sneaks out every night and brings the skunk baby
to her room. I've gotten so used to him scratching around
up there, it blends right in with the lullaby the crickets
chirp. There doesn't seem to be a thing in the world wrong
with that skunk that a few raisins can't fix. Margo has
named him Rabies.

Josh would rather pet Rabies than play catch or hide-
and-seek. He'll behave for thirty minutes at a time if he
thinks he'll get to play with that skunk. He's learned to be
gentle, but Margo still wants to be in charge when Josh
and Rabies play together.

She's in charge, period. She tells me how to hold Rabies,
like I wasn't the one that taught her how. She even bosses
Calvin—won't let him take Rabies with him back to the
barn. "He might wander off and get lost," she says. "I'm
the only one he minds."

She's right. Rabies can be halfway across the yard, and
if Margo calls, he'll turn and go to her. The rest of us can
call till we're blue in the face and he keeps waddling in the
other direction. No matter how crazy me and Josh and

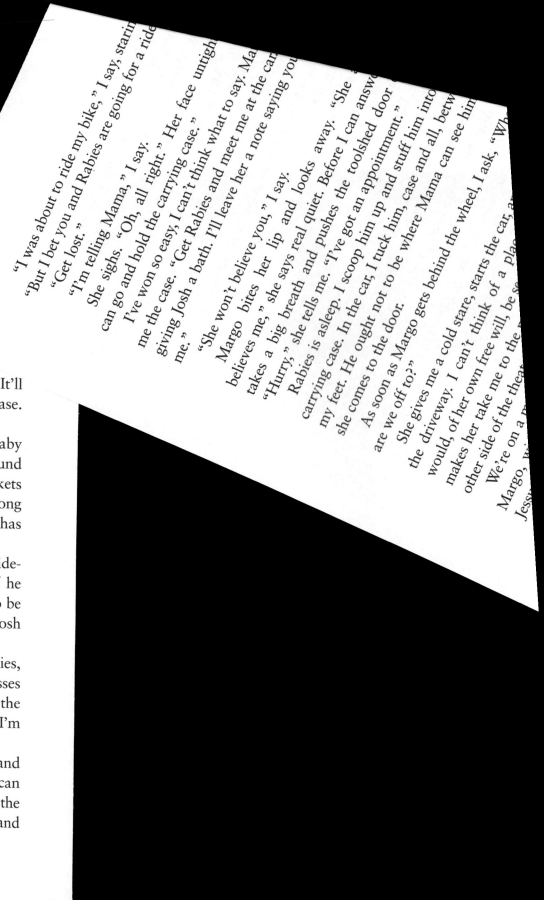

"I was about to ride my bike," I say, starin
"But I bet you and Rabies are going for a ride
"Get lost."
"I'm telling Mama," I say.
She sighs. "Oh, all right." Her face untigh
can go and hold the carrying case."
I've won so easy, I can't think what to say. Ma
me the case. "Get Rabies and meet me at the car
giving Josh a bath. I'll leave her a note saying you
me."
"She won't believe you," I say.
Margo bites her lip and looks away. "She
believes me," she says real quiet. Before I can answe
takes a big breath and pushes the toolshed door
"Hurry," she tells me. "I've got an appointment."
Rabies is asleep. I scoop him up and stuff him into
carrying case. In the car, I tuck him, case and all, betw
my feet. He ought not to be where Mama can see him
she comes to the door.
"As soon as Margo gets behind the wheel, I ask, "Wh
are we off to?"
She gives me a cold stare, starts the car, a
the driveway. I can't think of a plac
would, of her own free will, be s
makes her take me to the
other side of the thea
We're on a P
Margo,
Jess

I'm so worn out from going to doctors, building cages, and teaching Margo to tame a skunk, I go to bed without Mama having to say a word.

A racket jolts me awake in the night. Dogs are barking—Bo's bark in the garage mixed in with others. Somebody's running loud down the stairs. Daddy's hollering. The screen door slams.

I hit the floor practically running in my sleep. Just as I get to the back door, the BB gun pop-pops and dogs start yelping. Two strays slink down the driveway, their tails between their legs. One of them is limping. Bo is still barking nonstop.

In the floodlight Daddy's long shadow sprawls halfway across the yard. I run past him to the skunk pen. Calvin and Margo are already there. Margo is wringing her hands and whimpering while Calvin fiddles with the cage front where the wire is dented.

"Will you shut up?" he says to Margo. "They didn't get him."

Mama shows up carrying a half-asleep Josh. Daddy comes over and tugs on the cage wire.

"That'll hold till morning," he says. "You young'uns go on back to bed." He tucks the BB gun under his arm. "Those two strays won't be back for a while."

"Daddy, reckon they're the same dogs that got Margo's kitten and our hen?" Calvin asks. We had a hen that kept flying out of the chicken pen. Last week I found her bones and feathers in the barnyard.

"Probably." Daddy shakes his head. "I should'a used the shotgun." He and Mama and Josh start for the house.

Margo undoes the cage door and reaches into a back

corner for the skunk. She cuddles him under her chin, petting and soothing him. The skunk sets the ruffles on Margo's pajama top to trembling. "He's shaking like a leaf," she says. "Calvin, get me the carrying case."

Calvin stares at her and says, "You'd better not." I guess we both know what Margo has in mind.

"It'll just be for one night," Margo says. "Are you gonna get the case or do I have to?"

My room is right below Margo's. That little skunk's scratching is so loud, it sounds like he's beside my bed. It'll be a wonder if he doesn't worry a hole in the carrying case.

Margo sneaks out every night and brings the skunk baby to her room. I've gotten so used to him scratching around up there, it blends right in with the lullaby the crickets chirp. There doesn't seem to be a thing in the world wrong with that skunk that a few raisins can't fix. Margo has named him Rabies.

Josh would rather pet Rabies than play catch or hide-and-seek. He'll behave for thirty minutes at a time if he thinks he'll get to play with that skunk. He's learned to be gentle, but Margo still wants to be in charge when Josh and Rabies play together.

She's in charge, period. She tells me how to hold Rabies, like I wasn't the one that taught her how. She even bosses Calvin—won't let him take Rabies with him back to the barn. "He might wander off and get lost," she says. "I'm the only one he minds."

She's right. Rabies can be halfway across the yard, and if Margo calls, he'll turn and go to her. The rest of us can call till we're blue in the face and he keeps waddling in the other direction. No matter how crazy me and Josh and

Calvin are about him, Rabies is a one-human skunk. And that human is Margo.

I don't know if it was forgetfulness or on purpose, but this morning Margo walked across the backyard, in plain sight of Mama, with Rabies right behind her.

"Margo?" Mama called to her. "You remember what Dr. Jessup said?"

Margo kept walking. She bit off a chunk from an apple she was eating and dropped it for Rabies. That little skunk started eating the apple so delicate, it wouldn't have surprised me if he'd pulled a napkin out to wipe his mouth.

"That's a wild animal following you around," Mama said. "It's not our place to turn it into something else."

Mama warns me like that every time I bring an animal home. But my rabbit and dove and chipmunk were all hurt. I had to turn them loose when they got well. I still miss Ears.

When the two weeks are up and we turn Rabies loose, I'll miss him too. But Margo will miss him more.

After breakfast I head for the toolshed to get my bike. I'm reaching for the door when it eases open, just a crack, from the inside. Margo's left eye peers out at me.

"Go away." She makes it sound like a threat.

"Why?"

"None of your business."

Margo never sets foot in the toolshed. I open the door wide enough to scrunch in. She's holding the carrying case. "Whatcha gonna do with that?" I ask.

"I said none of your business." Her voice is shaky. She's got the same trapped look Ears had when I found him.

Margo kept the car today to go shopping. But she would never take Rabies with her on a shopping trip. Maybe I've caught my un-sneaky sister being sneaky.

41

"I was about to ride my bike," I say, staring at the case. "But I bet you and Rabies are going for a ride. Can I go?"

"Get lost."

"I'm telling Mama," I say.

She sighs. "Oh, all right." Her face untightens. "You can go and hold the carrying case."

I've won so easy, I can't think what to say. Margo hands me the case. "Get Rabies and meet me at the car. Mama's giving Josh a bath. I'll leave her a note saying you're with me."

"She won't believe you," I say.

Margo bites her lip and looks away. "She always believes me," she says real quiet. Before I can answer, she takes a big breath and pushes the toolshed door open. "Hurry," she tells me. "I've got an appointment."

Rabies is asleep. I scoop him up and stuff him into the carrying case. In the car, I tuck him, case and all, between my feet. He ought not to be where Mama can see him if she comes to the door.

As soon as Margo gets behind the wheel, I ask, "Where are we off to?"

She gives me a cold stare, starts the car, and eases down the driveway. I can't think of a place in this town she would, of her own free will, be seen with me. When Mama makes her take me to the movies, Margo sits clear on the other side of the theater. We meet at the car after the show.

We're on a main road, so it takes me by surprise when Margo, without so much as a signal, turns left into Dr. Jessup's parking lot. She pulls around the building and parks in back. "I'm getting Rabies de-scented," she says.

She comes around the car. I hand her Rabies' case and follow her without asking permission. She about bangs down the back door to Dr. Jessup's office. "He told me to come back here and knock loud," she says.

A woman wearing a smock with animals all over it unlocks the door. The second we set foot inside, she takes our carrying case, holds it at arm's length, and hurries down the hallway toward the little rooms. We follow, but when she opens one of the doors, she points us toward the waiting room.

"How long will the operation take?" Margo asks when the woman comes to the front desk. Her nametag says "Dora."

"I have no idea." Dora almost smiles. "This is his first skunk since I've worked here."

Dr. Jessup pokes his head through the doorway. "Margo?" He looks at her over his glasses. "Do you remember what I told you about a skunk's scent being its only weapon?"

"Yessir, I do." Margo stands straight and looks serious. "I'm a very responsible person, and I plan to take excellent care of Rabies."

When he hears Rabies' name, a smile flickers in Dr. Jessup's eyes, but it never reaches his mouth. "Does your mother know about this?"

Without batting an eye, Margo says, "Of course."

"You have her permission?"

"Absolutely," Margo says.

I feel my eyes getting big, so I blink a few times.

"Best I remember, she was set against you having this skunk de-scented." Dr. Jessup looks at Margo real stern. "What caused her to change her mind?"

Margo flutters her eyelashes. "Why, Dr. Jessup, I did." She smiles her flirtiest smile. "I can be extremely persuasive."

For a split second Dr. Jessup stares at Margo like he's a high school boy. Then he comes to himself and starts cleaning his eyeglasses with his coattail. "Well, I'm gonna de-scent your skunk for you—" He starts back down the hall, then says over his shoulder, "—now that you've convinced your mother."

When he's out of sight, Margo turns to me. "Shut your mouth," she says. I haven't said a word. She takes both hands to my nose and chin and eases my mouth shut. I don't know how long it's been hanging open.

Neither of us thought to bring a book, and, this early, there's no dogs and cats in the waiting room. I look at the tags on the different size collars, but they all say the same thing except for the prices. Margo snaps at me when I try to talk to her. She finally asks Dora for some paper so we can play tic-tac-toe.

We've changed to connect-the-dots and are on our third one when Dr. Jessup opens the hall door. Margo jumps up before he gets a word out.

"The operation went fine." He motions to her. "Come on back. I'll show you how to take care of your little friend while he heals."

Rabies is sprawled on white paper on the examining table. Margo lets out a little moan. Dr. Jessup chuckles.

"He'll come to in an hour or so," he says. Where the fur at the base of Rabies' tail is shaved naked, there's a stitched-up cut place. It isn't bleeding.

Dr. Jessup opens a tube of salve, rubs a dab on the cut, and hands the salve to Margo. "Three times a day, clean the area with peroxide on a cotton ball. Then put this on the incision." He gives her a small bottle of pills. "Give him one twice a day. Bring him back in ten days."

"How much do I owe?" Margo asks.

Dr. Jessup studies his clipboard. "How much do you have?"

The operation costs what Margo has saved up to buy a red winter coat. To the penny. She's going to bring the money with her when the stitches come out.

Dr. Jessup lines the carrying case with a clean white towel and lays Rabies on it real gentle. He looks over his glasses. "I'll call your mom. She needs to know what's involved in your skunk's recovery."

"Oh, that won't be necessary," Margo says. "I can tell her every little detail."

Dr. Jessup studies her. His mouth tightens into a line. He opens the door for us and says, "Bring him back in ten days."

When we get home, Mama is in the swing with Josh. She holds on to his shirttail until the car is parked. Margo opens her door to get out.

"Dr. Jessup phoned," Mama calls from the swing. "He was telling me about an operation he just did. One he thought I knew about."

Margo comes around the car, takes the carrying case from me, and starts toward the house.

"Aren't you heading in the wrong direction, young lady?" Mama's voice doesn't sound as mad as her words.

With no warning Margo explodes into crying. She stands with her back to the swing, stiff as a board except for when a big between-sobs breath shudders through her. "Please, Mama. Let me keep him in my room. He'll get germs in the pen."

Mama walks over and squats down to look at Rabies sprawled unconscious in the carrying case. She keeps a tight grip on Josh. I grab his other hand. He looks big-eyed at Margo, who can't seem to stop crying.

"Rabies dead?" he whispers.

"He can stay in the house a couple of days," Mama says to Margo. "But only a couple."

Mama digs a Kleenex out of her pocket, lifts Margo's chin up, pats at the tear streaks, and wipes Margo's nose like she does Josh's.

"I'm not used to being lied to, Margo," she says. "And I don't plan to get used to it."

Polly and J.B.

UNCLE MORRIS IS AUNT CORA'S HUSBAND. THEY LIVE IN TOWN IN A little house with almost no yard. That's why, when Morris bought a used pontoon boat at auction, he parked it in our pasture.

"First chance I get, I'll patch 'er up and get 'er outta here," Uncle Morris told Daddy.

After the hauling truck left, we all stood around eyeing the thing. I thought it looked nice, balanced on two long bulging floats in new spring grass. Sunrays bounced off the floats' silvery metal.

A clumsy wooden cabin sat at the back of the wide deck. I could squint my eyes and pretend that the cabin was the head of a giant silver-legged frog. The frog was hunkered down, staring at us with close-together cabin-window eyes. One jump and it would squash us all.

As Daddy studied the pontoon, a half smile broke out

on his face. "Kinda makes me wonder if it's hoping for a flood," he said.

"If I know Morris," Mama said, "that's what it'll take to get it out of here."

That was last March. Polly (my secret name for the pontoon) has stayed in our pasture rent-free for so long, Cora wouldn't take a dime for keeping Josh while the skunks were under our house.

Over a year away from water has been hard on Polly. Johnson grass and thistles are thick alongside her. A poison ivy vine has crawled clear up one float and is wrapping itself around the side rail. The paint has quit peeling and gone to falling off in chunks.

We're not supposed to go near Polly. And I don't mean to. But as I pass through the pasture on my way to the creek, Josephine sidles toward me with that thick head of hers lowered. In about two seconds, she's liable to get up steam and charge.

I run and jump high enough to grab the bottom bar of the rail that sticks out at an angle around Polly's deck. My shirt hikes up from the stretching. The sun has got the pontoon's wooden side hot as fire, and I about scorch my stomach pulling myself up. The deck floor is hot, too. I should have taken my chances with a cranky cow.

Usually Josie gets bored after she's had one of us cornered a few minutes. But she's munching on a tender patch of grass in Polly's shade. For the time being, I'm stuck.

I try the door of Polly's cabin. It opens without so much as a creak. A wave of heat hits me, but I ease in anyway.

Up close, the cabin is bigger than it looks from the ground—as big as a little room. It's clean but smells of smoke. Cigarette smoke, not the campfire type.

Along one side are bench seats that lift up for storage. One bench has narrow pull-out drawers underneath it. The top drawer is stuck. When I jerk it open, I find a tangle of fishing line, hooks, and a few floats. The next drawer opens smooth as you please. It has a *Playboy* magazine in it, a pack of cigarettes, and matches. And a pair of Calvin's glasses he claims he lost.

Finding this stuff is better than catching crawfish or seeing how many times I can walk the log across the creek.

The cabin's little windows are too high for me to see out without climbing. Before looking at *Playboy*, I sneak out the door to be sure I'm alone. Josie is staring toward the barn with her "Is somebody about to feed me?" look. She starts in that direction at a fast walk.

Whoever's got Josie's attention is liable to come as far as the pasture. There's no time for looking through the magazine. I'll have to settle for something to blackmail Calvin with.

The glasses won't do. They might break. I rip out the *Playboy* table of contents, fold it, and stuff it in my shorts pocket. Real quick, I find a picture of a nearly naked lady. I rip her out. Then I rip out three more.

I haven't been anywhere that I could get my hands on a *Playboy*. The naked-lady pages are my ticket to helping with minnows, tagging along on fishing trips, or doing anything else with Calvin.

I climb down Polly's side and head for one of my usual spots, the log that crosses the creek. Calvin comes whistling toward Polly. He probably can't see me through the trees, so I holler, "Hey, Calvin!"

He stops in his tracks and gets red in the face. Bo trots off, nose to the ground, following a rabbit trail. "What're you doing back here?" Calvin yells.

"What's it look like?" I jump off the end of the log and run toward him. "Wanna catch crawdads?"

"Mama's looking for you," he says. "And I've got to bait my minnow bucket."

Calvin keeps a metal minnow bucket lying on its side in the creek. He puts stale bread in it and leaves its hinged top open so minnows can swim in and out. If he needs fish bait, all he has to do is put more bread in the bucket. The minnows swim right in with Calvin standing there. When the bucket is just thick with them, he clangs the metal top shut. Those minnows are his for the taking.

I'm willing to bet the minnow bucket isn't his only reason for coming to the pasture. And that he's fibbing about Mama looking for me. But I leave without even begging to help with the minnows.

As soon as I get to the house, across one of the naked-lady pictures I write: "I've got the Playboy table of contents and more evidense." With the biggest safety pin I can find, I pin the page to Calvin's pillow, then tuck the bedspread over it sloppy, the way Calvin had it.

In my room I slip the table of contents inside a pair of panties at the bottom of my underwear drawer. Calvin would die before he'd rummage in there. Even if he opens the drawer, he'll never actually touch girl's underwear. I hide the other pages in the garage.

At the supper table, when everyone is eating and quiet, I ask Calvin, "How are those minnows?"

He pretends he doesn't hear.

"Your minnows okay, Calvin?" I ask louder.

"Uh-huh," he grunts into his plate.

"Calvin," Mama says, "is that a nice way to answer anybody?"

Calvin looks mean at me and says, "Uh-huh, Anybody."

Josh giggles.

"Boy!" I dip out a second helping of beans. "It sure takes a long time to feed a few slimy minnows."

"Honestly!" Margo says. "The subjects at our supper table make me want to puke!"

Josh makes a gagging sound.

"That's enough out of all of you," Daddy says.

After supper Mama sends me to feed scraps to the chickens. I throw a few bits of bread all the way across the pen. While the hens rush over there squawking, flapping their wings and quarreling among themselves, I sneak through the gate, dump the scraps on the ground, and am out of the pen before a single hen notices. I set the bucket down to fasten the gate. When I reach to pick it up, Calvin's shoes are there beside it.

"Where's that table of contents?" he asks.

I want to say something smart-alecky, but nothing comes to me. "It might be in my room," I say. I duck past Calvin and take off running so fast, I'm in plain view from the house before he can catch me.

It happens just as I thought. Calvin barges into my room asking for his property.

"You're welcome to search," I tell him.

He goes through my bookshelves and closet and the keepsake cigar box under my bed. Then he starts rummaging through bureau drawers. When he opens the one where the page is and sees all those panties, he closes it real quick.

I don't realize I'm grinning until I see him studying my face. Real slow, he pulls the underwear drawer open again. I feel my face change to worried.

"Whatsa matter, Jill?" Calvin eases the drawer open wider. "Thought you had me, didn't you?"

He picks up the panties I put on top on purpose—pink Sunday ones covered with little roses and lace. Calvin drops them on the floor. "I can read you like a book," he says. He starts flinging panties over his shoulder. "Always could." He finds the magazine page, crams it in his pocket, and starts to leave.

"Guess I'm the only thing you can read!" I say. "My note said I've got more pages. Other naked ladies!"

Calvin sits in a straight chair and glares across the room at me. "What do you want?"

I almost ask for a fishing trip. But he's already promised one of those for my helping with the barn.

I smile my sweetest smile. "I want to go with you to Polly whenever I feel like it."

"To who?"

I forgot he doesn't know my name for it. "Polly Pontoon. The boat in the pasture."

Calvin almost smiles. "We'll see," he says. "It'll cost you a page per visit."

"No, it won't," I answer. "You're not getting those pages back, no matter what!"

Calvin stalks out without another word.

"And I get to read *Playboy*!" I call after him.

Calvin'll probably burn that magazine. But I'll still have the torn-out pages.

Before I go to bed, I start a list of things to carry to Polly: the quilt at the back of my closet; a big pillow; my new comic book; candy corn.

Sharing the cabin of Polly Pontoon will be like when Calvin and I were together at our cave last summer.

No. It won't be like that. But at least the two of us will be there, together.

In my dream, Margo and Rabies and me and my rabbit are all the same size, dancing on our hind legs down a yellow brick road like the one in *The Wizard of Oz*. A pounding pulls me awake, out from under the covers, out of bed barefoot to the door and through, to the kitchen. It can't be Rabies in trouble again. He's still spending nights upstairs with Margo.

Some noisy man is hugging Mama just inside the back door. "Come on out here, Cliff!" he hollers in her ear. "The war's been over hell knows how long! I'm finally home!" He throws his head back. "Waaahhhh-hoooo!"

It's J.B. Walker. I remember the face where everything laughs at once.

Mama backs away, cutting her eyes at Daddy, who's stalking out of their bedroom tying his robe.

"I'll put on the coffeepot," Mama says.

Daddy tells me under his breath, "Go back to bed, Jill." But my feet won't move, and Margo and Calvin are crowding through the doorway behind me. Josh pushes his way between them, whining and rubbing his eyes.

J.B. flings himself at Daddy, grabs him around the middle, and hugs. The top of his head doesn't even come to Daddy's chin. Daddy wraps his long arms gentle around J.B. and holds him like he did me when the rock busted my toe. They stand glued like that. J.B. lets out a big gulping sob, but is dry-eyed and laughing when he backs away.

"Ain't you the damnedest sight for sore eyes!" He starts pounding Daddy's arm.

Daddy frowns and nods his head toward us. J.B. looks our way.

"They all done shot up like corn after a rain!" He picks up a round metal helmet that's on the cabinet by the door. "You, Calvin!" J.B. starts toward us and bumps into a chair that isn't in his way. "I brought you something." He puts his hand tight on Calvin's shoulder and gets steady on his feet. "I took this helmet off a dead soldier."

Calvin looks past J.B. for a sign from Daddy. Daddy nods, so Calvin takes the helmet.

J.B. moves right in front of me. I want to back away from his peculiar-smelling breath, but I stay put. He reaches across Josh to cup Margo's chin in his hand.

"Margo, you done got tall as me!" Saying it makes his eyes water. Margo is stiff. She smiles a smile I know is fake.

J.B. pats my hair. His hand is hot and shaking. "And Jill was knee-high to a grasshopper." He tries to squat in front of Josh and sits down hard on the floor. Josh scrunches back beside Margo and grabs her leg.

"Scaring my own namesake!" J.B. hugs his knees and looks up at Josh. The watery eyes spill over. "Don't grow up, son. They'll make a soldier out of you. They'll …"

Daddy bends, puts his hands under J.B.'s arms, and lifts him up. "Let's sit out in the swing," Daddy says. "Helen will have coffee ready in a minute."

I can barely remember us going to J.B.'s house when I was little. I could tell which was their driveway because their front yard had the most flowers. J.B. had a blond smiley wife and a boy named Bruce. We played together—even Margo—in a fenced-in backyard with a small furry dog. The grass was always cut.

J.B.'s voice was big then, too. He'd come whooping out

to where we were playing, tackle the boys, and fall in a laughing heap with them. He's the only grown man I've ever seen fall for the fun of it.

A morning coffee smell fills the kitchen. Mama has put sugar in one of the mugs. It must be for J.B. Daddy drinks his coffee black.

"You kids go back to bed," Mama says. "It's past midnight." She gets cream out of the refrigerator. "And Calvin. Leave that helmet down here."

"But, Mama! He brought it to—"

"You got no business with war things," Mama cuts in. "Leave it here."

J.B. is talking loud and hoarse in the swing.

"Margo, tuck Josh in, would you?" Mama checks the coffeepot. "He's asleep on his feet." She's talking loud, like that'll keep us from hearing the other.

"I don't see how anybody can sleep with a drunk in the swing!" Margo snaps.

Mama spurts over to Margo and grabs her by the shoulders. "Don't you ever say that again!" Her voice is shaking. "That's Cliff's best friend out there!"

Margo gives a little hiccup of surprise. Mama hugs her. "I'm sorry, Margo." She hugs her again. "Some men, when they first get back from a war ..." Whatever she's trying to tell us fades away. "Now go to bed."

So that's what J.B. is—drunk. It's my first time to see that, and I don't like it. Tonight's J.B. is out of kilter with the J.B. from my memory and from the stories.

Ever since I can remember, we've heard about Mama and Daddy and J.B. when they were young. Like the time J.B. met this new girl at a church social and talked to her a few minutes, then said, "Wait here. I got a friend you ought to meet." He found Daddy and told him, "I done picked you out a wife." He drug Daddy over to meet her. That new girl was Mama.

I'm about to doze off thinking about the long-ago J.B. when the right-now one lets out a loud laugh that jerks me awake. Margo was right about how hard it is to sleep when a drunk is in the swing.

Since the night J.B. showed up in our kitchen, I haven't heard a word about him. So it takes me by surprise when, at supper, Mama asks Daddy real cheerful, "So! How is J.B. working out at the plant?"

Daddy's face tightens mid-chew. He swallows, takes a gulp of iced tea, and mumbles, "J.B.'s not there anymore."

I didn't know he was ever there.

Mama asks, "You mean he got fired from just sweeping and cleaning?"

"It's a dangerous place." Daddy sits up straight and stops eating. "Everybody's got to be careful around those machines. Even the janitors."

Mama bristles. "Well, it seems to me they could've explained that to him."

"Helen." Daddy puts his fork on his plate and looks at Mama. "Last week J.B. didn't come to work for two days. When he did show up, he was so hung over, he passed out in a corner. We let him sleep it off. Next thing we knew, he'd woke up and started the lathe to running, not knowing a thing about it. He's lucky he didn't lose a finger before we got to him."

"Oh." Mama passes me the potatoes. "I still say whoever fired him could've—"

"*I* fired him!" Daddy's voice booms out. He pushes

back from the table and is out the door in almost one motion.

Mama goes after him. When I look around, Calvin and Margo and Josh are frozen like they're a snapshot of themselves eating supper.

Margo breaks the spell. "Calvin, did you know J.B. was working at the plant?"

"No." Calvin takes his plate and scrapes what's left into the scrap bucket. "But who else would hire him?"

Margo heads for the scrap bucket with her half-full plate. "I knew his wife kicked him out," she says.

Josh digs into his potatoes. I want to finish mine, but that would be like Josh instead of the others, so I pick up my plate and follow Margo. "Why'd his wife kick him out?" I ask.

Margo shakes her head at me and smiles at Calvin. He snarls, "Dummy." They disappear and leave me with Josh and the table clearing. I don't know whether to save Mama's and Daddy's plates or scrape them.

Mama comes back before I can decide. Her face looks puffy, like she's been crying. Daddy is right behind her. She gets a mug and heads for the coffeepot, talking fast to Daddy. "Al has that little house for rent. J.B. could live there. We can pay the rent if he doesn't."

"We'd be throwing good money after bad," Daddy says.

Steam rises from the coffee as Mama fills the mug. "I can fix lunches. You can take them to J.B. on your way back to the plant."

"It won't work." Daddy sounds tired, and sad.

"Well, it sure won't work if we don't try." Mama holds the mug up to him but doesn't let go. Daddy closes his hands around hers and takes a sip. She tiptoes to reach above the coffee and kiss him. Josh giggles.

"You two scat out of here!" Mama says. It's like they've just noticed us.

If Daddy hadn't taken lunch by for J.B. yesterday, Al's renter house would've burned down. When Daddy knocked, nobody came to the door, so he looked through a window. J.B. was passed out on the couch. Where he'd dropped a lit cigarette, smoke was coming out of some newspapers on the floor. By the time Daddy broke the window and climbed in, little flames were shooting up out of the papers, about to catch the couch on fire.

"I didn't have to call the fire department," Daddy says at breakfast, "but I did call Al. He's my friend, too. He can't afford to have that house burn down."

"Oh, Cliff." Mama sounds pitiful. "Where in the world will J.B. go?"

Daddy looks around the table before he answers. I think he's studying whether to speak his mind with us all listening. He turns to Mama and says for us all to hear, "Helen, we've never had a better friend than J.B., and we never will. But can't you see he's hell-bent on staying drunk?" He cups the side of Mama's face gently in his hand. "I can't watch any longer. We have got to let go."

Mama reaches up and pats Daddy's hand. He leaves quick, but not in a mad way. Mama gets up and glides toward the bathroom, sniffling and keeping her face where we can't see it. Josh scoots out of his chair and wanders toward his room.

"Damn," Calvin says under his breath.

I almost say "Don't cuss," but Margo beats me to it. Calvin ignores her. "I just keep remembering." He turns his tea glass round and round. "Back when Daddy thought

I was too young, J.B. took me to King Creek and taught me to gig frogs." He grins and shakes his head. "We sure had fun."

Margo snorts. "If you went frog gigging with him now, he'd probably stab your foot."

"Yeah," Calvin says. "Back then, he bragged about hard liquor having never touched his lips."

"Well, he's making up for lost time," Margo says. "Among other things, he's drunk himself out of a place to live."

Calvin starts fiddling with his fork. "There oughta be some way ..." He changes from turning the fork over to spinning it slow and thoughtful. He looks so sad, I decide to cheer him up.

"I bet we could save J.B. if we put our minds to it!" I blurt out.

"Who asked you?" Margo snaps. She looks hard at Calvin and says, "Don't pay her any attention, Calvin. If Mama and Daddy have given up, he's a lost cause."

"Maybe." Calvin doesn't sound convinced.

"J.B. is a wreck, Calvin," Margo says. She sits tall in her chair, gets a far-off look, and says in her breathy, poetry-reciting voice, "A wreck on the shore of life."

"You don't have to get sappy," Calvin grumbles.

"And you don't have to insult anybody who tries to talk some sense into your head!" Margo screeches her chair back from the table. "Or maybe you do." She flounces out of the kitchen.

"Calvin?" I talk fast before I lose my nerve. "What about Polly?"

He's twirling his fork around in circles on the table, not really listening. "What about her?"

"She's kind of a wreck, too. In the pasture, away from water and all." He's still not paying me any mind. "J.B. could live there."

The fork stops. Calvin looks at me like I fell out of the sky. "Yes!" He's up, out the door, loping toward the pasture. I'm right behind him, trying to keep up.

"We could sneak him food and he could take baths in the creek." I can't talk and run, so I hush after that.

When I climb up Polly's side, Calvin is already in the cabin, pacing off bed space. He's piled my stuff on the deck. It's a small heap. I never got around to lugging a quilt back here.

"I can bring my sleeping bag," he says. "And a couple of blankets."

"What about winter?" I ask.

"I don't care about winter," he snaps. "I care about tomorrow." He gets a pencil and tablet out of one of the drawers and shoves them at me. "Make a list. Soap. Drinking water ..."

After we finish the list, Calvin tells Mama he's gonna collect yard-mowing money, then sets out walking to the renter house to tell J.B. our idea. I'm supposed to ask for Margo's help finding the things on our list. But she's gone shopping with some friends. I'm glad. If Margo "helped," she'd take charge. Plus, the plan wouldn't be just mine and Calvin's anymore.

I figure soap's the most important thing. Anybody spending the summer in Polly's hot cabin is gonna need lots of soap. And deodorant. I dig out an old bottle of deodorant that's tucked back in the closet.

A new bar of soap might be missed. But Mama keeps the tail ends of our used soap in a big jar under the sink.

Once, she melted them down in a double boiler and poured them into Jell-O molds to harden. The soap that came out was rainbow-colored. I liked it. It took her so long to clean up the mess, she's never made it again. But she still keeps soap stubs, thinking she will.

I take four used soaps. In my bureau drawer, I find a toothbrush I used for only one week last summer at church camp. J.B. won't know the difference.

I don't dare take any toothpaste. Maybe J.B. will bring his own. In case he doesn't, I grab a handful of peppermints to tide him over until Calvin can buy toothpaste.

We need a jar to get drinking water from the barn faucet. I get an empty quart off the garage shelves where canning jars are stored. While I'm in there, I root around in a sack full of car-washing rags for clean raggedy towels.

Something hard is buried in the bottom of the sack. I dig out the helmet J.B. brought Calvin. Holding it and knowing where it came from gives me the creeps. But I don't put it down. It's like being afraid to see what happens in a scary movie but not looking away.

Mama whistles for me. I stick my head out and wave. She calls through the back door screen, "You got the clothes in, Jill?"

"I'm on my way," I answer. With all this collecting, I forgot my chores.

I cram the soap and what-have-you into the helmet, hide the whole business at the back of the garage, and head for the clothesline with a laundry basket. Calvin's coming up the driveway. He follows me, pretending to play with Bo.

"J.B.'s gonna try the pontoon," he says. "How's the list coming?"

"I did it by myself!" I brag. Calvin glares at me. Before

he can fuss, I add, "Margo's gone shopping. But I found the whole list. By myself."

"Well, that'll have to do for now." Calvin throws a stick for Bo to fetch. Bo plops down and puts his chin on his paw.

"I've got a plan, Jill," Calvin says. "A way to get the sleeping bag and blankets out to the pontoon right under Mama's nose."

"How?" I ask.

"That's for me to know and you to find out." He runs off, slapping his leg and calling Bo.

At the house I dump the clothes on the living room couch to fold them. Josh is coloring at the corner table. Margo is in the music room, practicing scales on her French horn.

Calvin comes through, headed upstairs with a half-eaten sandwich. He looks me up and down and hollers toward the kitchen, "Mama, make Jill change clothes." He glares at me. "Luther might stop by, and I don't want her looking like that."

I've worn this same halter top and shorts all day. They didn't bother Calvin till now.

Mama is just the other side of the door, stirring something on the stove. Without coming to look at me, she says, "Put a shirt on, Jill."

"Yeah, one that comes down to your toes," Calvin grumps. He goes into the kitchen. Josh giggles for no reason.

I keep folding clothes. When I get to Calvin's newest T-shirt, instead of folding it, I put it on. It comes down below my knees. Josh sings out, "Jill has Calvin's shirt on."

Calvin rages into the room. "You … ! You get that off

right now." His voice squeaks and croaks. "Mama, make her take my shirt off."

Josh sings, "Jill has Calvin's shirt on, Jill has Calvin's shirt on ..."

I stand tall. My toes look far away, down below the shirt hem. "You said ..." I wiggle my toes at Calvin.

"Mama!" he howls.

Calvin's acting so mean, it causes hot tears to rush up behind my eyes. I turn my back, so he and Josh won't see if the tears spill out, and keep folding clothes.

From the kitchen, in a voice like she's saying "Pass the bread, please" or "It's time to check the mail," Mama says, "Jill, take the shirt off."

"But, Mama, he said ..."

"Take the shirt off, Jill," Mama says again in a bigger voice; it ends the whole thing.

As soon as the shirt is halfway over my head, Calvin jerks it away and stalks up the steps, trying to jar the whole house. "Don't you ever touch this shirt again!" he bellows back at me.

"Fine!" I yell toward the stairwell. "I won't touch it when it needs hanging out." I'm crying now, and cramming folded clothes into the basket. "Or when it needs bringing in. Or folding. Or ..."

The French horn lets out a great blat, like some monster cow passing gas. Margo jerks open the music room door. The horn is tucked under her arm. "Would you all please act like human beings for once in your life?" she hollers. Then she calls toward the kitchen, "Mama, I've got a challenge to play. If I lose first chair, it'll be their fault!"

She spins around, slams the door behind her, and goes back to practicing triple loud.

Calvin is stomping around upstairs. Josh sings, "Jill wore Calvin's shir-urtt, Jill wore Calvin's shir-urtt ..."

I snatch up the laundry basket and go to put the clothes away. In the kitchen, Mama is humming something tuneless under her breath while she peels potatoes. I turn my head so she won't see I cried. "Remember to get a shirt on, Jill," she says real calm without looking up. "One of yours."

Calvin storms in from the living room with his sleeping bag and a blanket. "I'm not staying in the same house with"—he jerks his head in my direction—"with *that*." He stomps out the back door. "I'll sleep in the pontoon tonight." The screen slams behind him.

"You! Calvin!" Mama's voice stops him in his tracks. "You get back in here this minute." She looks at me standing there open-mouthed, tear streaks and all. "Jill, your job is to fold Calvin's shirts, not wear them." She turns to Calvin and tilts her head. "And you, young man. You apologize to your sister and put that sleeping bag right back where it belongs."

Calvin glares at a spot behind my head. "Sorry." It sounds like he's describing me.

Mama taps her foot. "You're trying my patience, Calvin."

He ducks his head and mumbles, "I'm sorry, Jill."

"That's better." Mama goes to the stove and starts cutting potato wedges. They make a steady rhythm, plopping into a pot of water.

I stare at Calvin, who's in the middle of the kitchen with a sleeping bag and blanket, staring at his shoes. Without looking up, Calvin asks, "Since I've got all this stuff together, can I go ahead and sleep on the pontoon tonight?"

We saved space in three drawers for J.B.'s things. I forgot to take the helmet back to the garage, so it's in a lift-up bench.

I'm on the deck arranging chiggerweed flowers and asparagus fern in a jelly glass when Bo jumps up, goes to the fence, and stands there wagging. He'd bark if it wasn't Calvin.

I hear talking before I see heads pop up over a rise in the Howells' pasture. J.B. spots me, throws his hand up, and hollers, "Wahoo! There's Jill! Hi there, pretty thing!"

The minute Calvin climbs on deck, he says to me, "You're supposed to be at the house." I don't answer.

All J.B. brought is the clothes on his back and a duffel bag. He's having a time climbing up with the bag, so I reach over to help.

"I'll hang on to that, little lady," he says, but I'm already hoisting it up Polly's side. When I set it on deck, the bag clunks. Calvin flinches at the sound.

"You ready to unpack?" he asks as J.B. climbs over the rail. The asking sounds like a dare.

J.B. winks at me. "I'll save that for when I don't have company." He picks up his duffel bag. "So this here's gonna be home for a while! Let's give her a look." He walks toward the cabin.

I open the cabin door, but Calvin doesn't move. "Whatcha got in that bag?" he asks.

"Private property," J.B. says. He's staring off into the trees.

"Want me to carry it?" I ask. They act like I'm not even there.

Calvin glares at J.B. "We had an agreement."

J.B. shrugs, unzips the duffel bag, and hands Calvin a

"Why?" Mama asks, but she's not paying much attention to anything but supper now.

"I don't know," Calvin says. "It's something to do."

Mama turns and looks at him. "Go on," she says.

He goes out the back door without once looking at me. By now I'm pretty sure that picking a fight with me was how Calvin planned to get J.B.'s sleeping gear to the pontoon. Maybe if I had figured that out sooner, the fight wouldn't have made me cry.

"Soon as you put the clothes up, Jill," Mama says, "set six places for supper, same as always. I know Calvin. He'll show up at mealtime, pontoon or no pontoon."

Sure enough, the minute Mama puts the last bowl on the table, Calvin eases in the back door and slides into his chair.

When everybody else is busy eating, he sneaks a wink at me. For some fool reason, his wink brings tears to my eyes worse than the shirt fight did.

I promised Calvin I'd stay out from under foot until he gets J.B. settled in at the pontoon. But that's easier said than done. After waiting as long as I can stand to, I let Bo out of the garage and we cut a trail for the pasture. Bo's so glad to be out, he circles and bounces like a young dog.

There's not a soul within shouting distance of Polly. Bo finds a spot in her shade and plops down. I climb up to check the cabin.

A straight chair we found in the garage, a crate that works as a side table, the sleeping bag—they all look downright homey. Jelly glasses, plates, and cups are in the tiny storage closet. I double-check the towel drawer, the soap and toothbrush drawer. Polly is stocked as good the motel room we stayed in for Cousin Betsy's weddin tall, square glass bottle. "I gotta have some whiskey now and then, Calvin," he says, real quiet.

"You said you was a changed man." Calvin's voice is doing the low-to-squeaky stuff. "A sober man." He takes the bottle and rears back like he's gonna throw it clear into next week.

"Calvin? I got to have whiskey to stay sober." J.B. isn't pleading, just saying. "Not a lot. Just some. I'm mostly dried out."

"Not on our property," Calvin says. "You knew that before you got here." He tightens his arm to throw.

"How about across the log?" I say.

Calvin freezes in his about-to-throw pose.

"Yeah, Calvin!" J.B. says. "Across the log sounds good." He turns to me. "Where's that?"

Me and J.B. hold our breath until Calvin lowers his throwing arm. He eyes J.B.'s duffel bag. "Cigarettes and matches, too, J.B. You promised."

J.B. studies his hands, then rummages in his bag and pulls out half a carton of cigarettes and two boxes of kitchen matches. I reach for them.

"We'd better review the rules," Calvin says.

Before J.B. sets foot in Polly's cabin, we come to a total different agreement from the one he and Calvin started with. Like in the first one, he agrees not to drink or smoke on the pontoon. I add spitting. No spitting.

The new part is, we hide his cigarettes and whiskey bottle in a hollow tree across the log on the other side of the creek. When he needs a smoke or a drink, he has to go over there.

The three of us balance our way across the log bridge. It's barely wide enough for even J.B.'s shoes. Once last summer

I crossed it running barefoot. It scared me so, I haven't tried again.

The creek bank is steep on both sides where the log crosses. Bo lumbers down on our side, wallows in the water till he's good and wet, and climbs the other bank. He shakes himself, flinging water on us as we step off the log.

"Durn if that ain't the most balancing I've done since basic training," J.B. chuckles. "Guess if I take one nip too many, I'll be over here till I sober up."

"Or fall in and get an extra creek bath," Calvin says. He smiles for the first time since he heard that bottle clunk on Polly's deck.

After supper, while Daddy and Mama are out for a drive and we're playing Rummy, Calvin says to Margo, "Check and be sure Josh is asleep."

"Who made you king?" she says. "If you want to know, go check on him yourself."

"Forget it." Calvin winks at me. "Guess we'll just keep our old secret."

After her next turn Margo lays down her cards and says, "I'm thirsty." She gets a glass of water, drinks it, and disappears toward Josh's room. When she comes back and plays her turn, she says, "Josh is asleep. What secret?"

Margo doesn't even try to hide how excited she is about J.B. "We've got a stow ... a ... way." She makes the word sound breathy. "This is so romantic. A real live stowaway! Like on a ship sailing the high seas!"

"He's on a pontoon, Margo." Calvin sounds almost as disgusted as if he was talking to me. "A pontoon in a cow pasture."

Margo's whole body stiffens. "Okay, Mr. Facts of the

Matter." She stands up, flings her cards at the table, and puts her fists on her hips. "How'd you like a dose of your own medicine? What we've got is not a stowaway on high seas or ..." She narrows her eyes at Calvin. "Or some little boy's hero." She lowers her voice to almost a whisper. "What we've got, Calvin, is a drunk!"

"Mostly dried out!" I say it good and loud. "J.B. said so."

Margo ignores me. "Furthermore." She marches toward the living room. "It's not 'we' that's got him. Leave me one hundred percent out of this!"

Calvin takes a deep breath. To the tune of Margo stomping up the stairs, he gathers up the playing cards. When Margo flung hers, some cards landed on the floor. I pick them up, hand them to Calvin, and say, "I'll one hundred percent help you, Calvin."

"Get lost," he mumbles.

The sun makes the pontoon cabin stifling hot during the heat of the day, so J.B. spends a lot of time outside. Sometimes he sits on the roots of our biggest oak tree and whittles. Every chance I get, I sit with him. I like to watch as his whittling knife changes what's just wood into birds and rabbits. And I like J.B.'s war stories. Which aren't exactly war stories.

"What's it like to shoot somebody?" I asked yesterday.

J.B. quit whittling. "As long as I'm telling 'em," he said, "I pick the stories."

So what I hear is not about shooting. And not about J.B.'s before-the-war family. Mostly I hear army-buddy stories. Once he told about teaching Calvin to gig frogs at King Creek. I acted like I didn't already know that.

This morning, I'm early. I climb up Polly's side and am

slinging my leg over the railing when J.B. comes out of the cabin, his shirt drooping over his pants. He's barefoot. It's the first time I've seen him sloppy. J.B.'s set on being clean—between the war and the drinking, he says, he's had enough nasty for a lifetime.

"Mornin', J.B.!" I say real perky. "I'm early."

He doesn't smile. "I ain't cleaned up yet, Jill."

"You look fine to me," I lie.

"Jill!" He says it urgent. "I know I'm on your property. But in them rules we made?" He runs his fingers through his hair, like that'll make him presentable. "We shoulda added, 'No girls on deck.' I gotta have me some privacy."

"Don't worry about me," I say. "And our only other girl is Margo. She couldn't climb up here if her life depended on it, so—"

"Tell you what!" J.B. laughs that big laugh of his. "Meet me at my whittling tree in an hour. I'll be rid of this five o'clock shadow."

"What's a five o'clock shadow, J.B.?"

He rubs his face. "It's what a man's face looks like when he needs a shave." He shoos me away with his hand. "Now get outta here, Jill. When you come back, I'll be spick-and-span." He looks up at the clear blue sky. "I been saving my favorite war story. This here pretty day looks just right for it."

It's not easy to sneak off twice in one morning. But with the promise of a war story, I manage it.

It's the best story so far—about this soldier pal that fell in love with a girl who couldn't speak a word of English. But when J.B.'s friend needed to hide, the girl hid him. A couple of years after the war—after J.B. quit being a prisoner and was in an army hospital—he found out his buddy married that girl. They came back here and live in Idaho.

I'm about to ask where in Idaho when Mama's "Come here, Jill" whistle sounds from the backyard. I don't want her coming back here looking for me and finding J.B., so I sprint for the house.

"Remember, Jill," J.B. calls after me, "no girls on deck." I'm almost out of hearing range when he adds, "Course, any gal totin' a T-bone steak's welcome!" His big laugh rings out so loud, I'm afraid Mama'll hear it.

Keeping J.B. fed is a job and a half. Every morning Calvin takes a sausage biscuit with him when he goes to milk Josie. Mama shakes her head and says, "Calvin, you're hollow to your toes!" J.B. has the biscuit and a glass of warm milk for breakfast.

Calvin buys peanut butter, jelly, bread, cheese, bananas, raisins, and such with his mowing money. I help him sneak the groceries back to the pontoon. Today, when J.B. sees us coming with the grocery sacks, his face laughs all over itself, like I remember from when we used to visit his real house and his real family.

"Whatcha got there?" He points at our sacks. "Reinforcements?"

"Calvin and Jill to the rescue!" I call out.

Calvin reaches the sacks up to J.B. When we start to climb up, Bo lets out a sigh and kerplunks down next to Polly.

The only extra thing J.B. has asked for, besides stuff to put on his bug bites, is mayonnaise. "It helps them sausage biscuits and cheese sandwiches go down," he said. "And if nothing else shows up, I can have me a may-yo-naise sammich!"

As J.B. pulls items out, he reminds us, like he always does, "When I get my next gov'ment check, I'll pay you back ever' dime."

"Well, when you get that check," Calvin says, "except for what you owe us, your money's going in the bank." It's like Calvin's the daddy explaining things to his overgrowed boy. "That money'll add up and you can move into a warm renter room, come the October frosts."

J.B. gazes at the groceries. "Reckon if I don't buy much hooch, I can afford a steak now and then?" He sighs. "And coffee. I miss coffee."

"You know a fire's out of the question," Calvin says. He sounds like the dad again.

"It's in the rules," I say.

Calvin looks at his feet. "Maybe when you get a check you can go for steak and coffee at Mel's Diner."

J.B. perks up. "Thanks for bringing this grub, son." He grins at Calvin. "You young'uns are mighty good to me. Don't pay my grumbling no mind."

On the way back to the house, Calvin says, "We need Margo. It's gonna take all three of us sneaking food to keep J.B. fed decent."

"Yeah, all three of us," I agree.

"I'll talk to her," Calvin says.

All three of us—me, Calvin, Margo. Taking care of J.B. is turning out to be almost as good as having skunks move in under the house.

In the shade of our biggest elm tree, Margo and Mama and me snap a bushel of pole beans into pieces about an inch long. Josh is at Cora's until the beans get canned.

While water's coming to a boil in the biggest pot we

own, I pick trash and dirt out of the beans. Then Mama gives them a good washing in the sink.

At the scalding-water part she shoos me out of the kitchen. I'm taking off for the pasture when Margo pokes her head out the back door.

"Oh, Jill?" she calls in her nice voice. "Wait for me. I want to take Rabies for a little stroll."

That makes no sense. Margo takes Rabies for walks all the time without saying "Kiss my foot" to me. I wait at the skunk cage anyway.

Rabies must've heard Margo. He's awake and pacing. He follows my finger along the cage wire with his wiggly black nose.

"Take me back to see J.B.," Margo whispers as soon as she gets to the cage. She reaches in, lifts Rabies out, and hugs him up against her.

"No need to whisper," I say. "I thought you hated the pasture."

She rubs her face against Rabies' fur. "I don't plan to live there, Jill. I promised Calvin I'd help with J.B. If I'm gonna sneak food for a stowaway, I have as much right to see him as anybody."

"That depends." I think up how to say what's bothering me so that Margo will pay attention. "I'm not gonna take you past Josie and shoo snakes so you can be snooty to J.B."

"What makes you think I'd do a thing like that?"

"The way you're all the time calling him a drunk, for · one." I say. "He's mostly dried out."

Margo bats her eyes at me. "I'll be sweet as pie."

She takes Rabies with us. When we get to the barn lot, Josie is grazing in the holding pen. Her watering trough's in there, so it's one of her favorite places.

Margo says, "Jill, why don't you pen that cow up so I won't be a nervous wreck the whole time we're back here?"

I check to be sure there's fresh water in the trough, and fasten the holding pen gate with Josie still in there.

Margo says she wants to see where J.B. lives. I show her my skinned knees and tell her, "You'll have to climb the side of the pontoon."

"Forget it," she says.

The scabs on my knees aren't from climbing Polly's side; I didn't exactly say they were. But with Margo thinking it, there's no need to tell her about J.B.'s no-girls-on-deck rule. If she knew about the rule, she'd find a way to break it.

J.B. is under his tree, whittling. By the time he notices us, we're pretty close. He gets a wild, about-to-run look. Then he leans down, throws his knife hand up in the air, and hollers, "Bless old Bess! I got company." He stands up and brushes the wood shavings off his pants legs. "Two pretty girls done come to pay me a visit."

"Two pretty girls and a skunk," Margo sings out, and holds Rabies high in front of her.

"Whatcha whittling?" I ask. J.B. blows sawdust off the figure he's working on, wipes it clean with his shirt, and holds it up. A dog's head, front paws, and part of a body are sticking out of a small chunk of wood.

"Why, that's Bo!" Margo squeals. "It looks just like him, J.B." She reaches over to finger the ridges in wooden Bo's fur. "How'd you do that?" She gives J.B. a big-eyed, flutter-lashes look.

"I always did take to whittling," J.B. says. "It passes the time."

"Tell Margo about your army buddy that fell in love with the foreign girl," I say.

"Ahhhh," Margo kind of purrs. She sets Rabies on the ground and points at me. That means I'm to watch her skunk instead of listen to the story. She settles herself on a big tree root, bats her eyelashes at J.B., and asks, "Is this story romantic?"

"It's so romantic," says J.B., winking at me and grinning at Margo, "I could tell Hollywood and be rich for life."

He settles back against the tree trunk and gazes into space. "I first met this fella—Charlie was his name—in a bar ..." Margo stiffens. "Uhhh, in a barber shop on the base where we was both stationed ..."

Margo and J.B. don't even notice when I leave to rescue Rabies, who's disappeared under some blackberry bushes. I lure him out with ripe berries. If Mama could see Rabies gobbling those berries, she'd say he's hollow to his toes, like Calvin.

I set Rabies in a clear spot to begin his exploring. He pokes his nose into tangles of grass and follows trails like a dog. Whenever he starts toward bushes or a fencerow, I head him off. My arms already have scratches from the blackberry briars. I don't want more wounds from chasing somebody else's skunk.

We come to a big log that's been on the ground rotting ever since I can remember. Rabies sniffs at it, gets excited, and starts ripping one spot to shreds. Big ants pour out of the hole Rabies is making. He eats the ones that get on his paws and keeps tearing at the log.

When Rabies gets to where the ant eggs are stored, he slurps them up, along with whatever ants try to stop him. He wipes out an entire generation of that anthill without stopping for breath.

I figure that, with a full stomach and his skunk habit of

sleeping during the day, Rabies is ready for a nap. I snuggle him up against my shirt, and he doesn't try to wiggle free.

I head back to J.B. and Margo, walking slow and easy, hoping to lull Rabies to sleep. Maybe I'll get to hear the story's end.

Margo is leaning against the tree trunk, gazing up at J.B., her mouth half open with listening. J.B. laughs. "'You done got it bad,' I told Charlie when he come back to the barracks all moon-eyed." He looks down at Margo. "He loved that little gal from the moment he laid eyes on her." J.B. gets caught up in looking at Margo. "She was such a pretty thing ..."

Some invisible magnet moves his fingers to barely touch the side of Margo's face. She flinches but doesn't swat his hand.

In a trembly voice I can barely hear, J.B. adds, "Like you, Margo. A tender, pretty young thing. Waiting for her life to happen."

A breeze lifts a wisp of Margo's hair and feathers it onto J.B.'s hand. They're frozen there, Margo gazing open-mouthed at J.B. and him looking hypnotized down at her, his hand gentle on her face.

A mockingbird starts singing. It's like I'm watching a movie with a bird singing background music. But Margo and J.B. ought not to be in it.

I say loud and clear, "This skunk's wore me to a nub." Margo and J.B. jump like I've thrown a lit firecracker at them. "It's time somebody else ..." I look down at Rabies, who barely stirred when I spoke out. "Well, what do you know? Rabies has wore himself out, too." I can't stop chattering. "You ready to take over, Margo? I sure am tired of skunk-sitting, and ..."

Margo jumps up, brushes off the seat of her walking shorts, and hurries over to me. Her face is as red as I've ever seen it. "Sweet baby," she says, easing Rabies out of my arms and folding him to her where her shirt swells out.

Rabies stirs in his sleep again. Margo wraps her arms around him and coos soft nothings, planting little kisses in his fur. Her hair falls like a curtain. There's very little skunk showing.

Margo's acting so sweet, it makes my stomach flutter. I turn to smile at J.B. His eyes are locked on Margo. Hypnotized still.

All at once, J.B. shuts his eyes and rubs his face with one hand like he's trying to get rid of something. He looks up with that same need-to-run look he had when we surprised him while he was whittling.

"Margo sure loves Rabies," I say to him in a voice that comes out louder than I meant. "That's one lucky skunk."

J.B. stands and says to me, like Margo can't hear, "It's time Margo and her lucky skunk went back to their house."

Margo flips her hair back. "Rabies had a nice outing, and we're both utterly exhausted." She aims her best smile at J.B. "Thanks for the story, J.B. I'll hear the ending when I don't have a skunk to tend to."

She heads toward the house, using a floaty walk she learned in ballet class.

"She can't be ex-haust-ed," I say. "Margo's just saying that to use big words. I've kept up with Rabies practically ever since we—"

J.B. stands up, still watching Margo. "Jill." He says it so gruff, it scares me. "You know how the story ends. Finish telling it to Margo. She's got no business coming back here again."

"It's okay, J.B." I try to smile like Margo. "You tell the story a lot better than I could, and I don't mind getting her past Josie whenever—"

"It's not okay, Jill." J.B. reaches like he's gonna take me by the shoulders, then backs off a step. "Listen to what I'm telling you! You're welcome back here. But don't bring Margo." He waves me away. "Go on home now." He walks past Polly and heads for the creek log. "And finish that story for Margo."

As soon as I get to the house, I tell Margo what J.B. said. She plops down on the couch and crosses her arms. "It's our pasture, and I'll go back there anytime I feel like it."

I come back with, "The only reason you wanna go again is, somebody asked you not to." I jump into the story, trying to imitate J.B.: "Charlie brought that gal to Idaho and ..."

Margo stops up her ears. "Nobody but J.B. Walker is gonna tell me the rest of that story, and that's final." She stomps up the stairs to her room. I'm hot on her heels till she slams the door in my face.

"This wouldn't have happened," I yell, "if you hadn't paraded your flirting ways!"

Mama's head pokes out of Calvin's room. She's got an armload of dirty sheets. "What wouldn't have happened?" she asks. "Who's Margo flirting with this time?"

"N-nobody." I back away. "The same old boys at church."

Mama knocks on Margo's door. "Margo?" she calls. "What's going on?"

Margo opens her door and glares past Mama at me. "Nothing that a certain brat minding her own business wouldn't fix."

"Maybe this *is* my business, and Margo's poking her nose in it!"

Mama sighs. "If you two are going to argue all summer, at least you could find something worth arguing about!" She heads for the steps.

As soon as Mama gets out of hearing range, I start where we left off. "One thing's sure," I say under my breath. "If you go where you're not wanted, you're on your own with Josie."

"So?" Margo narrows her eyes. "I'll watch till that stupid cow is in the holding pen and then shut the gate, like you did." She slams the door in my face and hollers through it, "Who needs you?"

Sunday. A day of rest. As we pile into the car after church, Daddy grins and says, "Looks like a King Creek day!"

So that's why Mama stayed home. To get things ready.

The smell of fried chicken meets us halfway between the driveway and the house. We herd through the kitchen. Mama says, "Hustle into your creek clothes. We'll eat when we get there."

King Creek is my favorite place. Today I'm double glad we're going. It'll give me a break from tracking Margo. If she decides to sneak back to the pasture, there's no way I can stop her. But if she goes back there, I'll go, too.

To save time and trouble, I put my swimsuit on under my shorts and shirt. I grab a book, a towel, jeans, and last year's sneakers. When I get to the car, Margo and Calvin have the trunk open. Margo is loaded down with lotions and magazines and nail polish bottles. She's trying to cram her radio in next to our ice chest. "Why are we carrying all this junk?" she asks Calvin.

"Beats me." He fits her radio in. "I've got no use for nail polish."

Amidst all the fishing poles, minnow nets, tackle boxes, what have you, there's barely trunk room for my spare shoes.

The screen door slams behind Josh. He's lugging goggles, flippers, a beach ball. All he has on is swim trunks. They ride low beneath his little poochy-out belly.

Margo runs to claim the front seat window. I climb in the back. A couple of pairs of waders are in the floorboard where my feet need to be. Extra clothes are already piling up between me and where Calvin will sit. It's a good thing something's separating us. The minute Margo began helping with J.B.'s food, Calvin got over being nice to me.

"Here, Jill!" Mama plops a bulging sack in my lap. "Hang on to this. It's lunch." A hot fried-chicken smell fills the car. Mama settles Josh to my left and climbs in under the steering wheel. Margo gets to stay by the window.

"I just had a brainstorm," Margo says. "Let's take Rabies with us!" She opens the door and goes tearing toward the shed before Mama can answer.

Calvin opens the back door on his side and rams two frog gig poles toward me.

"You're gonna put my eye out!" I holler. "Mama, make Calvin put those frog gigs in the trunk!"

"I already tried," he growls. "They won't fit."

"Calvin," Mama says, "the handles will have to fit up here one way or another. But take those sharp gigs off first. They're small enough to fit in the trunk."

Daddy comes out of the house and hollers, "Everybody in!"

Margo comes hurrying through the yard with Rabies in

the carrying case. "Jill?" She smiles at me and sets the case in Calvin's place. "There's no room up front, so could you please ..."

"That's your skunk, Margo," Mama says. "If it goes with us, you'll hold it and you'll watch it. All day."

I cross my eyes at Margo. She mouths "Pest!" at me and grabs the cage. Rabies loses his balance and lets out a little squeal. Margo studies where she's gonna sit up front, then stomps back toward Rabies' pen.

Calvin threads the poles between Margo's place and Mama up front, then between me and his spot in back. He gets in, yanks his door shut, and plasters himself against it, careful not to touch me. Daddy has the motor running when Margo comes back without Rabies. The car eases down the driveway.

Before we're even to the road, Josh starts bouncing his beach ball off the lunch sack, crashing himself into me every time he catches it.

"Will somebody pleeease make Josh behave?" I beg.

King Creek is calm. Getting there isn't.

Our spot on King Creek is tailor-made for us. There's this wide, flat stretch of creek gravel where Margo lies on her beach towel to get a tan. Daddy and Calvin don't have to wade far upstream to reach deep fishing holes. Next to where we park the car, the water is clear and shallow, born to be waded in. It empties into a spot deep enough that Josh can splash around trying to swim, but shallow enough that Mama can wade in to rescue him without soaking her walking shorts, unless she wants to.

Before Daddy gets the trunk open, Josh is in the water.

"You stay in the shallow part," Mama hollers at him,

"or the goggles and flippers stay in the car."

It's already steamy hot along the creek bank. The air is thick with the smell of wild roses. Calvin sheds his shirt and flings it in the back seat with the spare clothes. Daddy takes off his long-sleeved khaki shirt and adds it to the pile.

"Jill?" Mama says. "You and Margo lay out the lunch. It'll spoil in this heat if we don't eat now."

The fried chicken is still hot. When I open the wrapping, its smell draws Calvin and Josh.

"Mama's not gonna let you and Josh eat with no shirts on," Margo tells Calvin. He goes to the car, scrambles through the clothes, and brings back his shirt and one for Josh. Daddy gets out the cooler, and Mama passes everyone an icy Nehi grape drink.

When the rest of us start cleaning up the picnic leavings, Josh says, "Now for some fun!" and trots toward the wading water.

Down the creek a blue jay squawks. Another answers from somewhere in the woods. The day stretches in front of us, drawing us like the chicken smell pulled Calvin and Josh.

Daddy and Calvin disappear upstream with their fishing gear. Margo arranges her nail polish bottles down one side of her towel. Mama saunters along the shore, looking for wildflowers and berries and keeping an eye on Josh. I follow along with Mama awhile. Off and on, we gather wood and stack it for the night's campfire.

As an excuse to wade without looking babyish, I help Josh find shells and pretty rocks and periwinkles. I catch a few crawdads and put them in his bucket. He likes to lower the bucket into the water and let the crawfish float out one at a time. He's scared of their pinchers. When he gets big enough not to hurt them, I'll teach him how to catch crawdads from behind. That's the surest way. They mostly swim backwards.

Mama lets Josh get in his swimming hole, so I find a lonesome willow where I can dangle my feet in the water and read *Stuart Little*. Once in a while, I just sit, letting creek and bird sounds swirl over me like the water lapping my feet.

Before time for the air to start cooling, I wade upstream to where the creek's barely deeper than I'm thick. There, I shed down to my swimsuit and lie down in the water with my head on a rock in the shallow part. I try not to move, breathing slow to keep my stomach from jiggling.

Minnows bounce nibbles off my legs, but I don't twitch to scare them away. The current goes right over my stomach, not noticing I'm new. I stay still long enough for crawfish to think I'm a rock and scoot under my back. It isn't the tickle of their crawling I like. It's the stillness, the turning into a quiet thing, being a solid place in the world.

I feel something that might be an old crawdad; a bullfrog upcreek lets out a *charugg* that ends with a question mark, like he isn't sure it's time to tune up yet.

"Jill," Mama says far away and soft. "Time to get out. It'll be dark before you know it." She's afraid we'll catch our death of cold, being wet after dark in creek air.

I'm at the car, drying off but still wet and shivering, when Daddy and Calvin get there. Daddy hands Mama a string of bluegill and frying-size catfish. She gets pliers and a knife and heads downstream to dress the fish. Josh is napping in the back seat.

Frogs up and down the creek begin answering the first one. The air settles around us, darkening fast like when they dimmed the funeral home lights before Mrs. Dunn's burying.

Daddy puts his khaki shirt back on and leans against the car's front fender to pull on his waders. Calvin is at the trunk, pressing the little pitchfork-looking gigs onto their long poles. I sidle over to Calvin and talk like Luther would.

"Man, listen at them frogs, Calvin!"

He stops and listens.

"I can taste frog legs now!" I rub my stomach. "How many you gonna gig?"

Calvin stands tall and looks toward the creek. "It's a good night for it," he says. "We oughta get more'n all us put together can eat at one meal."

Before I can think of any more Luther-talk, what pops out is, "Can I go?"

Calvin glares at me. He's woke up to who he's talking to.

"I'm fast," I say. "I could catch ever' frog I chase ..."

"Sure, Jill," Calvin says. "Come with us and chase frogs." He calls over to Daddy, "Might as well leave the sacks here, Daddy. Jill's going with us and chase frogs." He gives a disgusted grunt and walks off toward the creek.

"Come here, Jill." Daddy's voice has a chuckle in it. Maybe he'll let me go.

"We don't chase frogs," Daddy says. He aims his flashlight at a rock about the size of a baseball. "Bless old Bess! There's Mr. Bullfrog now! Watch how this beam of light hypnotizes him." Daddy presses on the rock with his gig. "All I gotta do is pin him to the mud so he can't take off, then reach down and pick him up."

He picks up the rock and shows it to me. "See there?" He turns it over. "Didn't even break the skin." He pretends to put "Mr. Bullfrog" in his tow sack. "Gotta keep 'em alive until time to dress 'em or the frog legs are no good."

Daddy musses my hair and heads for the creek.

"I can do that," I say, following right behind him.

"Not tonight," Daddy says. "We're getting a late start. Tell your mama it'll be dark night before we get back." He and Calvin, loaded down with gigs, tow sacks, and long-handled flashlights, slosh-slosh away from me up the creek.

I bet if J.B. was here he'd teach me to gig frogs, no matter how late it was. In no time I'd be as good a gigger as Calvin is.

Mama comes back and puts the dressed fish in the cooler. We build a fire and start roasting hot dogs while Margo reads by flashlight. Mama puts the first roasted hot dogs on buns and wraps them up for Daddy and Calvin. The smell wakes Josh. Margo quits reading, stretches, and asks, "Can I help?"

I hand her a stick I've burnt the hot dog crud off of. "Thread some marshmallows on here," I say.

Something howls far away. "I'm ready to go home," Margo says.

Mama gives Josh a couple of barely browned marshmallows. He gulps them down, then comes and leans into my shoulder until I about lose my balance.

"Jill, I want your 'shmallows," he begs in sleepy baby talk.

I catch my marshmallows on fire and don't blow them out until they're total black.

"They burnt," Josh whines.

"That's how I like them," I say. Josh goes back to Mama. I hold my marshmallows away from the fire. Their blackness mixes with the night.

"I'd better find a flashlight," Mama says. She gets up and rummages in her pocket for spare car keys she keeps on a knotted shoestring.

About the time Mama finds her flashlight in the trunk, Josh says, "I gotta pee." He trots out into the bushy darkness.

"You wait for me, young man!" Mama slams the trunk down and takes off after Josh, her flashlight beam doing a crazy dance from the jolts of her running.

"I'm liable to have to go in the bushes in the dark, too," Margo grumbles. She starts gathering up her things. "I wouldn't have come if I'd known we were gonna be here half the night."

I stay by the fire, burning marshmallows and blowing them out. Margo sets her bundle by the car. When Mama and Josh get back, she says, "Mama, I need the trunk key."

Mama fishes in her pocket. "I can't find it." She checks again. "It's locked in the trunk, sure as the world."

Margo nudges her lumpy towel with a toe. "I'll just leave this here till Daddy gets here with his key."

Mama comes back to the fire, shakes her head, and grins. "Cliff'll never let me live this down."

"Mama, I gotta go," Margo whines, "and I'm afraid to go by myself."

"Margo's scared to pee-ee, Margo's scared to pee-ee!" Josh chants, skipping around.

While Mama's gone into the darkness with Margo, long watery sloshes come our way in the creek. A beam of light flicks and disappears.

I tell Josh, "Something woolly is coming to get you." He wads himself up in my lap and puts his hands over his ears. Circles of light bob on the water as Daddy and Calvin

"I knew that would happen," Margo says. She begins singing softly to Josh.

Daddy opens the driver's side door and Mama scoots in under the steering wheel. As she settles herself next to Margo, Josh crawls into Mama's lap. "The bugs are just awful out there," she says.

Calvin opens the back door. Across the top of the car, Daddy tells him, "Leave the gear for now. But you'd better [get] those frogs in here."

Margo wails, "Frogs in the car? With me?"

"You wanna babysit 'em outside?" Calvin asks. "Shoo the coons, the snakes, maybe a bobcat?"

Margo stops up her ears.

"Hush, Calvin!" Mama says.

Margo makes a big to-do of propping her book up so she can read. Nobody says a word to her about flashlight batteries. Calvin puts both sacks of frogs on floorboard on his side. Josh clambers from Mama's lap into the back seat. I catch him before he falls on the floor.

"see the frogs," he says.

"Hush!" Daddy says. "Sit still and be quiet." To Mama, he says, "If we don't find the keys pretty soon, I'll into that trunk."

Mama gets on her feet and puts her arm around Daddy's. He's gripping the steering wheel with both hands. "We got no money for repairing the trunk lock," Daddy says. "..."

They're mumbling to each other. I plant Josh on my lap. With mallow-sticky hands he pulls my head to him and whispers in my ear, "I wanna see the frogs." I poke him with my elbow. The frogs are wiggling

wade closer. By the time they clear the creek, Margo and Mama are back.

"Got any frogs?" Mama asks.

"There was so many," Calvin says, "we coulda just held our sacks open and let 'em jump in."

Josh scuttles out of my lap and runs to see the frogs. Calvin sets his sack down and opens it for Josh. I run over and look, too.

There are probably forty frogs in Calvin's sack, crawling all over each other. Whenever one scrunches up to jump out, Calvin spreads his hand so the frog hits his palm and falls back onto the others. Josh reaches two fingers in and gently touches a frog. I poke my hand in. The frogs feel soft and cool. Each one we touch freezes, barely breathing until we move to another one.

Calvin lets us pet the frogs awhile. "I gotta help Daddy," he finally says. Josh tries to sneak a frog out of the sack.

"Put it back," Calvin says.

"Wanna frog."

I pull Josh out of the way. Calvin wraps a fish stringer around the sack top, ties it in a double knot, and sets his sack next to Daddy's. Both sacks thrash around like something big and mean is in them.

Josh squats down and puts his hand on one of the sacks.

"You, Josh!" Daddy hollers from near the campfire. "Get away from there." Josh jerks back like he's touched a hot stove. But he keeps looking at the sacks.

"Cliff," Mama says real sweet, "how about opening the trunk so we can pack up?"

Daddy gives Mama a puzzled look as he reaches for his keys. "I thought you had keys."

"I do." She sidles up to him and puts an arm around his

waist. "I did." She lays her head on his shoulder. "They're in the trunk."

Mama is all tucked up against Daddy's side. He grins, lifts her chin, bends down like he's forgot everything except her being available to kiss. We're all watching.

"The kids, Cliff," Mama says. "The keys."

Daddy kisses her light and quick, straightens up and slaps at his shirt pocket, digs in it and comes up empty-handed. He tries the pocket on his T-shirt, then his pants pockets front and back. "They're gone," he says.

Margo lets out a moan. "I'm not staying in these mosquitoes another minute!" She flounces over to the car, gets in the front seat, and slams the door.

Josh giggles and heads for the creek. Mama swoops down on him. "Miss Margo can entertain you," she says. She goes and dumps him in Margo's lap. "Read to him, Margo. Josh, you stay put." She goes back to Daddy and asks, "Now what?"

"I'm pretty sure my keys were in my shirt pocket." He puts both hands on the hood of the car and bows over it in a whipped-looking way. By and by, he straightens up. "Calvin, get everything ready to load. Your mama and I will figure something."

"We passed a house a little ways back," I say. "Can't we walk up there?"

"No, Jill," Daddy says. "You walk up to a house around this neck of the woods at night, you're asking to get shot." He hands me his flashlight. "Make yourself useful. Search around the car."

I crawl all around the car, moving rocks that are big enough to cover Daddy's keys. Calvin takes the gigs off the poles and adds them to what's waiting for the trunk to open.

"Hey, Calvin," I whisper. "This is like be wrecked. Maybe we can just live here."

"Dumbbell."

"No, I mean it. We got food and …"

"Hey, Mama!" he yells. "Jill wants to li

Mama comes over to me. "Jill, this isn' under her breath. "Your daddy's worrie

I hand her the flashlight and stand We've got food, and clothes, and ma

Mama stops me with, "—and Cl to milk, animals to feed."

Me and Calvin look at each feeding animals reminds me o Calvin's thinking, too. We've haven't given J.B. a thought groceries. He probably has mayonnaise sandwich, si

Calvin takes his ligh searching for the keys

"Jill, not another get in the car and k

"But I wanna k

"Get in the c

I crawl into Margo's not flashlight?" against th reading. Calvin way.

"(teries.

against my right foot. "Frogs, Jill?" Josh whimpers.

"Shut up and be still," Calvin grumbles. He shoves the mound of clothes in my direction, turns to face the window, and leans his head against the seat back. To get away from Josh I balance cross-legged on top of the pile of clothes. As I settle in, Josh lunges for the frogs. He grabs a sack and pulls the stringer. Its knot starts unraveling.

Josh scrunches down in the floorboard. "Wanna see the frogs," he whispers over and over, tugging at the stringer.

From my perch, I nearly fall over trying to loosen his grip. "Calvin!" I say low so Daddy won't hear and blame me. "Help!"

Calvin whirls around. He makes a sleepy, off-target try for the sack. Josh pulls harder. The stringer uncoils fast like a startled snake. The sack flops open. I'm looking down into a puddle of frogs.

A frog inches out and crawls away. Calvin grabs for it. Josh giggles and turns the sack bottom up. Frogs tumble every which way.

One frog jumps onto Josh's lap; the front legs of another are on his knee. They're crawling all around him. His giggles turn into cackles as he picks a frog up and holds it against his face.

"What's the commotion back there?" Mama asks from some other planet.

"Frogs," I say.

Daddy shines his flashlight bright on us. "What in tarnation?"

Josh lifts his frog up and yells, "Margo! Look!" When Margo turns, she's eyeball to eyeball with Josh's frog. She lets out this deep animal moan and opens her door so fast she about falls out. Croaks and insect chirps flood into the car loud, like they're coming through some giant megaphone. Margo starts having a heebie-jeebie fit outside the car.

"Shut that door!" Daddy yells. "Where's the sack, Calvin?"

I'm on my knees, wobbling around on top of the clothes. I hand Daddy the sack and bend to look for frogs. One swats me in the face mid-jump. It's like there's a million of them scooting under the front seat, crawling into shoes, jumping up, and disappearing under the pile of clothes.

With their flashlights, Mama and Daddy spot frogs for me and Calvin to catch.

"We've got most of 'em," Calvin finally says. I'm trying to pry Josh's frog out of his grip. He starts howling.

"You gonna kill that frog, squeezing so hard," I say through clinched teeth. Josh eases his grip a little, but hugs the frog up against him so I can't get to it. "His liver's gonna ooze out through his eyes and get all over you."

Daddy reaches down to where Josh is. "Turn loose, son," he says. Josh goes limp and Daddy takes the frog. There's not much spark left in it.

"You all finish up," Mama says. "I'll tend to Josh." She opens the door to the night sounds again. Margo is leaning against the front of the car, whimpering and swatting at mosquitoes.

Mama opens the door on my side to get Josh. "Frogs!" he blubbers.

"Frogs, my hind foot!" Mama lifts him out of the car, wraps a jacket around him, and shuts the door.

Calvin about stands on his head to search under the front seat. "I see another one!" He slaps the floorboard and scares the frog to where Daddy can catch it up front. Nothing else moves.

I hand Daddy the fish stringer and he ties a complicated knot. "Jill, you check the clothes," he says. "If you find a frog, take it to the creek. This sack is closed for the night." He hands me a flashlight. He and Calvin get out.

I pick up shirts and pants one at a time, shake them, look them over by flashlight, then throw them in the floor. The last thing is a T-shirt I had on over my bathing suit. When I pick it up, my light glints off something shiny in the crack of the seat. I drop the shirt and ease my hand under the shiny object.

"Yaaay!" I yell. "Look what I found!" I tumble out of the car. "The keys! I found the keys!"

Waving Daddy's keys to make them rattle, I run over to where he's squatting by what's left of our fire. Mama is standing near him, rocking Josh side to side. Daddy stands and rubs his face. When I hand him the car keys, he goes, "Shhew-wee!" It's more a relaxing than a word. "Where'd you find 'em?" he asks.

"Under the clothes I was setting on."

Mama looks up at Daddy. "Bet they fell out when you threw your shirt back there."

"Hawp!" Daddy's "get cracking" whoop is so loud, Josh jumps in his sleep. Margo and Calvin come running. Daddy meets them halfway to the trunk, dangling the keys for them to see. "Load up!" Daddy says. The three of them scurry around the car, laughing and making lots of happy going-home noises.

To smother the fire, I kick sand over it. "If it wasn't for me"—I glare at Mama and kick harder than I need to—"we'd be here all night. Is this all the thanks I get?"

Mama is swaying back and forth with her head resting on Josh's. She smiles. "You mean," she asks real soft, "after S-E-T-setting on those keys all this time, you want thanks for finally hatching them?"

Cousin Hershel

I BRING IN THE MORNING MAIL. MAMA SHUFFLES THROUGH IT, sorting out the bills, until she gets to a royal blue envelope. She opens it first. As she reads, worry lines show up on her forehead. She mutters, "Lord help us all, I'd better get busy," and jots something on the writing pad she keeps handy for grocery lists.

She notices me still standing there and gets this lost look, like I'm somebody she met a long time ago and can't quite place. Finally she says, "Jill?" She picks up the letter and waves it at me. "Soon as the dew's gone, let's see if we can find enough blackberries for a couple of pies. My cousin Hershel is coming for a visit."

Mama's kin are pale, educated people. They don't visit us much. When they do, Mama scrubs and carries on and gets out a tablecloth. We stay out of her way.

I've never met the one that's got her in a tizzy this time.

Hershel. I'm glad his letter didn't get here a few days ago and knock us out of our King Creek time.

The way Mama's flitting around, it's easy for me to disappear long enough to warn J.B. that we're coming to the pasture to pick berries. He says he'll walk to town.

When I get back to the house, Calvin has left to mow Mrs. Thompson's big yard and Mama is dressed for the berry patch.

Margo asks her, "Why don't I keep Josh here at the house?" She's hoping to get out of picking. She hates wearing the hats and long-sleeved shirts and old jeans that keep blackberry briars from scratching us to pieces.

It works. Mama lets Margo stay at the house with Josh.

Near the pontoon there's a blackberry thicket that's higher than Mama's head. It's so loud with the buzzing of June bugs and bees feasting on its berries, it sounds like a low-flying airplane got caught in its brambles.

The first berries ping into our tin pails. As the pails fill up, those pings change to thunks. We pick without talking. Birds call to each other. I take time out to catch a June bug and set it on my open hand. Its coarse sandpaper legs feel like tiny scratchy fingernails. It tickles its way to the edge of my palm, takes off, and flies away.

Out of the blue Mama says, "Lord only knows what condition Hershel will be in." She hardly ever uses the Lord's name in vain. It's happened twice since she opened the letter.

My second bucket is barely half full when Mama starts her third. She rolls her shoulders around, stretches as high as she can reach, and says, "Think I'll take a break. As little rain as we've had lately, I've been meaning to see how low the creek is."

I'm in such a rhythm of picking, I don't stop when Mama's low whistle for me adds itself to the buzzing sounds. She whistles again, so I set my bucket in the shade and head for the creek. Mama is squatting at the water's edge, studying some footprints. "Look." She points at a half-empty jar of mayonnaise that's wedged between two rocks.

J.B.'s mayonnaise. He keeps it cold in the creek.

"Must be a tramp," is all I can think to say.

"If that's the case," she says, "he's settled in. Whoever owns that mayonnaise plans to use it again." She stands and gazes up and down the creek bank. I cross my fingers and toes, hoping J.B. hid the army helmet good. He uses it to dip up water when he takes a creek bath. If it's poking out of the bushes, Mama will recognize it for sure.

"I don't know if we ought to finish picking," Mama says. She keeps looking around like she wonders if we're being watched. "I'd better go to the house and call Cliff."

"Calvin's back here a lot," I say. "Let's ask him if he's seen anybody."

Mama heads toward the berry patch. I get a brainstorm and run to catch up with her. "I betcha it's Calvin's jar! Remember those biscuits he takes with him to milk? And … and how he brought his sleeping bag to the pontoon? He probably eats back here all the time." I take off toward Polly. "Why, I'll just climb up that old boat and see if his stuff's still there."

"No need, Jill," Mama calls after me. "I'll ask Calvin. We've got enough berries. Let's go to the house."

As we start for the barn, she says more to herself than to me, "Calvin doesn't put mayonnaise on sausage biscuits."

Giggles are coming from the orchard. The weeds and bushes in the fencerow are so thick, we can't see through. Mama breaks into a trot toward the gate. I spill a few berries, trying to keep up.

As soon as she can see into the orchard, Mama's shoulders relax. Margo, in her swimsuit, is posed on a beach towel in a sunny spot. Josh is in the shade of a peach tree, leading Rabies around and around with an apple slice.

Seeing us, Margo calls, "Josh was fussy at the house."

I hold up a pail. "The berries are ripe. There's billions of 'em!"

Margo loves blackberries. She jumps up and slings her towel over her shoulder, saying, "Time's up, Josh. Rabies needs a nap, and so do you." She scoops Rabies up and holds a carrot chunk for him to nibble. Josh starts to fuss.

"You be nice and we'll do this again soon," Margo tells him. The noise stops mid-whine.

There's no chance to tell Margo about the mayonnaise jar. Calvin's the one who needs to know, anyway. When he gets back from mowing, I'm waiting at the toolshed to warn him.

"I'll convince Mama it's my mayonnaise," he says while he puts up the mower. "But we'd better tell J.B. to be more careful about keeping stuff hid."

By suppertime, the whole house smells like blackberry pie. But all we get is sandwiches. The pies are for when Hershel gets here.

One good thing: Mama's mind is so filled up with Cousin Hershel, he must've crowded out the mayonnaise jar. At supper she doesn't say a word about it to Daddy.

I clear the table while Daddy finishes his coffee. "You'll have to mind your p's and q's," Mama warns me. "No loud noises. Cousin Hershel just got out of the hospital, and his system needs to adjust."

Josh comes ripping through the back door, pretending he's a motorcycle. He makes braking noises and crashes at Mama's feet. She closes her eyes and just stands there, then says, "Hershel isn't used to children. Maybe I'd better ask Cora about keeping Josh."

Daddy heads for his easy chair in the living room. "Don't you go shipping our kids off," he says, "to accommodate somebody fresh outta the loony bin."

"Cliff!" Mama gives me her you-didn't-hear-that look. "Hershel's always been delicate. He can't help having a nervous breakdown."

Daddy grunts. "His nerves can't stand the thought of his inheritance running out. He might have to make a living, like the rest of the world."

There's not gonna be a single spider left in the corners of our house when Mama and Margo get through cleaning it for Hershel. They even did my room, and Mama never lets company see in there.

My job is to keep Josh out from under foot. I've started taking him and Rabies to play in the orchard, like Margo did. Today, when we get back in sight of the house, there's a long man sitting in a cloth folding chair in the shade of our backyard maple. A little serving tray Mama saves for company is beside him. I've never seen that tray outdoors before.

"That must be Cousin Hershel," I tell Josh. "We've got to be quiet." He giggles. I add, "You'd better behave if you want to play with Rabies again."

I put Rabies in his pen, try to brush some of the grass off Josh's shorts, and arrange his sweaty hair as best I can.

Mama comes fluttering out the back door. She's got a big glass of iced tea and a magazine.

"Wanna hug Mama!" Josh whines. I latch on to his shirt. If I turn him loose, he'll run grab her around the waist and make a big commotion. "Walk!" I tell him.

As we get in hearing range, Hershel says, "That does look inviting, Cousin Helen. But tea sets my nerves to twittering." He turns slow-motion mournful eyes toward us. "Are these yours?"

Mama looks at Josh like she wishes her answer could be no, and that she hadn't listened to Daddy about calling Cora.

"This is Jill," she says. "And Josh. Margo and Calvin will be home directly." Sounds to me like Mama hopes the other two will make up for having to introduce us first.

Hershel gives us a far-away half smile and makes a funny puffing noise through his nose. He reaches for the magazine Mama brought. His hands look scrubbed and polished. I've never seen such long, beautiful fingers on a man *or* a woman. "A gardening magazine?" He barely turns a page. "I've never read one."

"They're soothing," Mama says. She's studying Josh, like maybe there's some way she hasn't thought of to make him disappear. "I'll get ice water," she says.

"No ice, please, Cousin." Hershel sniffs again. "It goes right to my head."

I'm staring as bad as Josh. Here it is the middle of the week, and Cousin Hershel has on Sunday pants and shirt and shoes, and smells like the tonic his hair is slicked back with. He's not paying us any mind, just thumbing through the pages of flowers, raising his eyebrows once in a while.

At the back door, Mama calls in a sugar-coated voice,

"Jill? Josh? Come wash up and I'll fix you a snack."

Josh is so hypnotized, I have to practically drag him away from Hershel. "He staying long?" Josh asks in a loud whisper. Cousin Hershel sniffs.

Mama gets a glass out of the cabinet, holds it up to the light, gets another one. "I'm just not used to delicate anymore," she mutters. She turns on the faucet and lets it run, tests the water and fills the glass. "Jill," she says, "you keep Josh quiet. When this blows over, I'll make it worth your while." She heads out the door with the water.

I don't know how or what time Cousin Hershel got here, but Mama's in such a state, I make up my mind to ease things for her the best I can. Halfway through our snack I tell Josh, "You be good and I'll let you play with Rabies again."

"Now?" Josh crams what's left of his bologna sandwich in his mouth and grabs his milk glass. He's out of the chair before I say, "No, dummy. You gotta be good first."

"Today?" he begs.

"Tomorrow, Josh," I promise. "You be good today and you can play with Rabies after your nap tomorrow."

Margo and Calvin come in with sacks of groceries. Mama tells Margo right off, "Honey, Cousin Hershel will be spending a few nights, and I've given him your bedroom. While Cousin's outside, you'd better get some clothes for tomorrow."

Margo glares at me like this is my fault. "Give him Jill's room," she says. "I need mine."

"Nobody else's is nice enough." Mama sounds desperate. "Just move some clothes to Jill's room. Hershel won't be here forever."

"Mama ..." Margo wails.

"The subject is closed," Mama says.

Margo stomps out and up the stairs. When she comes back down, I'm in my room, waiting. She takes one look at the pallet Mama put in the far corner, dumps her stuff on my bed, and barges out. In no time she's back with clothes on hangers. She opens my closet door, squishes my clothes to one end of the hanging bar, and arranges hers so they'll hang free and not wrinkle.

Margo turns and sees that I've moved all her stuff to the pallet. She starts moving it back to my bed.

"This is my room!" I say in my meanest voice. "That bed you're piling junk on is my bed, and you can't have it."

"A total stranger has taken over my room," Margo snaps. "If I have to move to this pig sty, I'm not about to be more miserable than I have to be." She picks up a shirt I've worn only once and holds it out like it's a stinky dead varmint. "Has anybody ever explained to you the purpose of our dirty clothes hamper?"

I storm out to the kitchen. "Mama, Margo thinks she can have my bed! Make her move to—"

"Shhh!" Mama says. She glances toward the backyard. "You're making enough racket to wake the dead! Just be glad you've still got your room. Let Margo sleep wherever she wants to."

Mama has me set Cousin Hershel's place at the supper table between her and Daddy. It's like she thinks Hershel needs shielding from us kids. I wonder if Daddy's gonna do his part.

When Hershel sees all the bowls of hot vegetables and the fried chicken, he sniffs real loud. After the blessing, Mama starts the bowls around.

I'm in charge of Josh, but he's working so hard for another chance to play with Rabies, I don't even have to remind him to chew with his mouth shut.

Margo's still mad about the room, but she tries to be a lady anyway. "I've always wondered, Cousin Hershel," she says in her fanciest voice, "what is Paris like this time of year?"

"Different," Cousin Hershel says through a mouthful of mashed potatoes.

"Different?" Margo says, real polite.

"So is hell," Daddy says.

"Cliff!" Mama squirms in her chair. "Why don't you pass the homemade rolls to Cousin Hershel?" She pats Hershel's arm. "They're Cousin Sarah's recipe. You may have eaten them when she was able to cook."

"May have," Hershel mumbles as he scoops out seconds of creamed corn.

"He's had three already," Daddy says. "You don't need another roll, do you, Hershel?"

"Believe I do." Cousin Hershel stares at the plate of rolls until Daddy offers it to him. He takes two.

After supper Hershel goes up to Margo's room, comes back down with a leather travel bag, and locks himself in the bathroom.

"I never saw anybody eat so much," Margo says. "Not even Luther." Every time Luther eats with us, Mama declares he's gonna bust.

Cousin Hershel stays in the bathroom a good thirty minutes. Margo bets Calvin a milkshake that it'll be dark before he comes out. Finally Daddy knocks on the bathroom door. "Hershel, the kids need to get ready for bed," he says. Mama tries to shush him, but he adds, "Your time in there is up."

There's considerable clunking and shuffling in the bathroom before Cousin Hershel comes out in a dark blue silky-looking robe. His hair is slicked back. He smells like the after-shave counter at McLellan's.

Josh giggles, then claps his hand over his mouth and cuts his eyes toward me. He's already earned Rabies, and I can't blame him for giggling, so I give him a smile.

"I shall retire for the night," Cousin Hershel says. "Pleasant dreams, everyone." He looks at all of us except Daddy.

Mama scoops up Josh and heads for the bathroom to get him ready for bed. Calvin picks up the Authors cards. "Take those cards outside," Mama tells him. "And don't get near Cousin Hershel's window."

"You mean Margo's window," Margo grumbles.

We put a blanket down under the catalpa tree. Calvin sets his camping flashlight at an angle so, if we hold them just right, we can see our cards.

"What does 'retire' mean?" I ask Margo.

"Go to bed," she says.

"But you said I could play, and ..."

Margo stops me with a look. "You asked what 'retire' means, Jill. It means 'go to bed.'" She shakes her head. "Some people ..."

Calvin grunts. "If that old windbag's re-tired, I think I'll call him Cousin Retread."

"Why?" I ask.

"Whatever you call him, Calvin," says Margo, "it was pitch dark when he got out of the bathroom. You owe me a milkshake."

"Why you gonna call him Cousin Retread?" I ask again.

"Tires, dummy." Calvin draws a card and lays down a pair of Nathaniel Hawthornes. "Retreads on tires."

We've finished the first game before I finally figure out what Calvin means.

"*Re*-tread!" I say. "Redoing a tire! Re-*tiring*." I fall sideways on the blanket giggling. "That's a good one, Calvin!"

He couldn't look more disgusted if I'd thrown up on him.

"It's past your bedtime," Margo says. "Why don't you—" She smiles at Calvin. "Jill! Why don't you retire?"

Calvin deals just two hands. His, and Margo's.

Ever since Cousin Hershel got here, it's been easier to sneak food for J.B. Whatever disappears, Mama figures Hershel ate it when her back was turned.

While Josh is down for his afternoon nap, I wrap up a leftover chicken wing in a napkin, stuff it into my shorts pocket, and head for the pasture. J.B. is at the blackberry bushes, eating berries as he picks them. Josie is close by. It's got to where she hangs around J.B. like Bo hangs around Calvin.

When J.B. sees me, he throws his hand up in a big wave. "Come join us, Jill!" He motions toward Josie. "Me and Miss Josephine are grazing." He pulls an extra-big berry off a high limb and hands it to me. "Yessir. Living off the land. Mighty fine eating." He sniffs the air. "Hmmm. Unless my nose fools me, this here berry patch is beginning to smell like fried chicken."

I grin and pull the wrapped-up wing out of my pocket. "Here's why."

"Time's a'wasting!" J.B. wipes his hands on a clump of grass. "That smells too good to eat standing up. Let's go sit in the shade."

On the way, J.B. picks a big catalpa leaf. At our tree, he

lays the leaf on the ground between us. "Now ain't that the finest shade of green you ever saw on a china plate?" He breaks the wing into pieces, arranges them on the leaf, and looks at me. "I'm obliged to share."

"No thanks, J.B. I just ate."

"Well. If you're sure."

I nod.

He takes a small bite and closes his eyes while he chews. He swallows and grins at me. "Fine eating."

I try to arrange myself on the tree root graceful, like Margo. J.B.'s got his eyes closed again, like it'll shut out everything but the taste of home-fried chicken.

"Margo wouldn't listen to me finish your army-buddy story," I tell him. I'm not sure he's paying attention, but I keep talking. "I didn't get the first sentence out. She said nobody but J.B. Walker is gonna tell her how that story ends." I giggle. "If we weren't in such a swivet over Hershel, she would've snuck back here already."

He opens his eyes and looks at me before he takes another bite. "So Margo won't abide by my druthers?"

"That's the way she is." I point to a rabbit that's taken the first hop out of some bushes. "Now that she's seen how I fastened Josie in the holding pen, she's gonna do that and come back here all by herself."

The rabbit sits up and looks around, then makes a bee-line for a big clover patch. J.B. goes back to eating chicken. When he's about finished, I tell him, "Hershel could've polished off a whole chicken by now."

"Hershel don't know how to appreciate fine food," J.B. says.

"That's all he does know how to do—appreciate food. And get waited on. Mama waits on him hand and foot."

J.B. flings the last bone as far as he can throw it and licks his fingers. "Sounds like a prince of a fella."

"Well, I hate having a prince in our house! We have to be quiet all the time because of his nervous condition. And Margo's the boss of my room. It's just the awfullest way to live ..."

I could bite my tongue for saying that. I can tell from J.B.'s eyes that he's reading my mind like Calvin does. But I say what's on it anyway. "I'm sorry, J.B. Fussing about room sharing to somebody who's living on a pontoon in the middle of nowhere."

"Why, this here pontoon"—he waves toward Polly— "it's the best kind of home. Specially since it's equipped with nice young'uns to take care of a fella." He gets this light-dawning look. "You know what, Jill? Getting took care of by that family of yours gets to be habit-forming." His "remembering" look takes over his face. "Your dad's took care of me one way or the other since ... why, since I wasn't much older than you are now!"

I smile at him, knowing a story's on its way.

J.B. leans back against the tree trunk. "Yessir. First time he laid eyes on me, two bullies had just ripped my school shirt and tore the pages outta my notebook." He looks off into the distance. "Here come Cliff, who didn't know me from Adam's uncle. He was about Calvin's age, and so were the bullies."

"Bet he beat 'em up good, huh, J.B.?"

"Wasn't no need, Jill. He just come and stood next to me. They slunk off. He called after 'em, 'You, Junior! And you, Tom! This young'un needs a new notebook. Needs it by tomorrow.'" J.B. smiles at the remembering. "That notebook was on our porch next morning."

"So my daddy rescued you?"

"And became a friend for life." His voice gets close to him and wispy. "But Cliff's wrote me off. Can't say as I blame him." He stands up quick and starts toward the creek. "I need to wash my hands."

I call after him, "I'm glad you like our pasture, J.B." Halfway to the barn, I turn back and holler, "But I'm not glad Cousin Hershel likes our house!"

Hershel is in that same canvas chair he brought with him, flipping through the same magazine. The water glass on the side tray is half empty.

Josh meets me at the back door and says, "Rabies."

"Right after our snack," I say.

Mama is putting a roast in the oven. I tell her, "Josh has been so good, I'm gonna let him play with Rabies."

She sits down beside Josh and smooths his hair like she doesn't even know she's doing it. "That's fine. Just stay back there around the pen." She lets out a little under-her-breath laugh. "If Cousin Hershel gets sight of Rabies, I'm liable to have to serve up cooked skunk."

Josh turns to Mama and starts howling.

"Shhh!" She hugs him to her. "I was just kidding, Josh. Just kidding."

As me and Josh walk to the skunk pen, I call out real perky, "Hello, Cousin Hershel." He barely lifts one eyebrow, and doesn't look up. "You old Retread, you," I mutter under my breath.

Rabies hears us coming and rears up on the mesh wire, begging to be petted. "Let me help get him out," I say. I place one of Josh's hands under Rabies' stomach and one over his back. When we lift him out of the cage, the sharp claws flail mid-air but don't scratch us. Josh hugs Rabies close, then sets him on the ground and leads him around with apple chunks.

I brought *The Secret Garden* to read. I sit cross-legged in the grass and find my place. Once the apple's gone, Josh lies down and lifts Rabies onto his stomach. Every time Rabies tries to get down, Josh sets him back in the middle of his T-shirt.

I'm reading one of my favorite parts—where Colin walks for the first time—when Josh says real quiet, "Jill?"

"What?" I don't look up.

"Jill." Josh comes up behind me, puts his arms around my neck, and leans. I almost lose my balance. "Rabies is bored of me."

I look up to see Rabies waddling toward the house. I could chase him down before he gets to Cousin Hershel, but I don't. I just watch, ready to run if Rabies gets in danger.

Cousin Hershel lays his magazine on the little side table, yawns, and stretches. He picks up the glass of water and eases it to his mouth. Those slow eyes of his gaze real lazy over the glass rim as Rabies strolls by his chair.

Hershel stiffens and his eyes grow. "God A'mighty!" he yells. He spills the water all down his front and starts trying to roll himself out of the chair, whimpering worse than Josh ever has. "Helen!" he yells. "Help me, Cousin Helen!" Hershel's chair folds up with him in it and tumbles over toward Rabies.

Rabies may not have any scent, but he has the instinct to use it as if it was still there. He turns his rear end toward Hershel, stomps a quick little dance with his hind feet, and hikes up his tail. Hershel clambers out of the chair and half crawls, half runs toward the house, moaning and yelling and spluttering.

The commotion brings Mama to the back door. "Why, Cousin Hershel!" She holds the screen open wide for him. "That's just Rabies."

He moans louder and crashes past her into the house.

"That skunk's been de-scented," Mama calls as the bathroom door slams behind Cousin Hershel. Mama holds her apron up over her mouth. Her eyes look like she's about to bust out laughing or crying.

Margo pulls up into the driveway. I flag her down and point to Rabies. She jumps out of the car and runs toward him.

"Oh, Margo." Mama dabs at the corner of her eye with her apron. "Poor Cousin Hershel thought a real skunk was after him." She lets out half a giggle, then claps her hand over her mouth, like that'll keep the other half in.

Margo squats and calls Rabies. He trots right up to her, behaving total different from a minute ago's scared skunk.

"Doesn't anybody care," Margo snaps, "that my sweet baby is loose in the yard, about to get run over?" She snuggles Rabies under her chin.

Mama dries her eyes and pats at her hair. "I'd better go check on Hershel. Poor fella."

Mama coaxes Cousin Hershel out of the bathroom, but he goes straight upstairs.

At suppertime, Hershel won't come out of Margo's room. Mama takes his supper up to him on a tray. But she doesn't take him seconds.

Our garden is bearing like there's no tomorrow. Mama is meeting herself coming back, waiting on Hershel plus trying to can vegetables. Without actually admitting it, we're all pitching in above and beyond our usual chores. Margo has taken over the laundry except for Hershel's clothes. His first day here, he made arrangements with Akin's Cleaners to pick up and deliver his laundry. He must have money to afford that.

Me and Calvin are doing double time in the garden, weeding, watering, picking whatever's ready. Sometimes I take Josh with me. He can entertain himself in the dirt a long time with a shovel and bucket and his toy bulldozer.

Today we picked lima beans. Again. We've got a big mound of them on newspapers in the middle of the living room floor. Whoever's in there shells beans. Even Josh has his little bowl to shell in.

Hershel doesn't help. Last night Calvin handed him a bowl of beans to shell and said, "Don't want you to feel left out, Cousin." Hershel looked at all of us looking at him. He picked up a pod like he was afraid it might bite him, worried it open, and got four beans out, one by one. Then he stretched, yawned, and said, "These long summer days just wear a body out." He set the bowl of beans on the floor and disappeared up the steps.

Margo's in my room this afternoon, so I'm looking for somewhere else to be. When we're in there together, it's more like a battlefield than a room. I wander into the kitchen. Mama's drinking a cup of coffee while Josh eats apple slices with peanut butter smeared on them and raisins stuck in the peanut butter.

Before I sit down, I check to be sure Hershel's in his lawn chair. Nowadays we don't spend much time at the table unless he's outside. The last time me and Margo and Calvin played Monopoly in the kitchen, Hershel and

Daddy were in the living room reading. We started laughing. Hershel called out, "Can't you kids be quiet a minute?"

Daddy came barreling through the kitchen. "I'm going for a ride," he muttered, "before that freeloader who's ordering my kids around gets a black eye." He slammed the screen behind him. Calvin began putting the Monopoly back in its box.

"Why're you doing that?" I asked.

"Old Retread can have the whole durn house," Calvin said. So we went outside and played cards.

I'm about to fix myself an apple–peanut butter–raisin snack when Calvin comes in from the garden. He washes his hands and gets out fixings for a bologna sandwich. Margo saunters in and pours herself a bowl of cereal. I get cereal, too. Margo points to the bananas. Josh makes car noises as he steers one across the table to her.

"Oh, Cousin Helen!" Hershel calls from the yard. "Would you have any ice cream in there?"

Mama's fingers tighten around her cup. She calls through the screen door, "I think we've got a little ice cream, Hershel."

"A spoonful would sit well about now," Hershel calls back.

"How long are we gonna put up with Old Retread?" Calvin asks.

"He's family, Calvin." Mama heaps ice cream into a bowl. "None of his other relatives are healthy enough to take care of him till he recuperates."

Once she's out the door, Margo says, "I'm gonna send Hershel a whole box of get-well cards."

When Mama gets back, she tells us, "That ice cream

was supposed to be supper dessert. Jill, soon as Josh is down for his nap, let's pick blackberries." She sighs. "They're going to waste. Maybe we can salvage enough for a couple more pies."

Margo comes to attention. "Mama?" she says. "You're just worn out. You take a nap with Josh. I'll help Jill pick blackberries."

Mama stares at Margo. "That's tempting, but ..."

I feel my mouth hanging open. If Mama goes picking, there's no time to warn J.B. If Margo goes, it'll break my promise to J.B. to keep her out of the pasture.

Mama looks at Calvin. "Would you go with them, Calvin?"

He grunts; it passes for a "yes."

Hershel is asleep in his chair, with his long, bony legs sprawled out so far, they look pulled like taffy. It's a mystery to me how he stays skinny as a beanpole. All he does is sit and sleep and eat.

My banging the berry pails together wakes him. He stretches. I sing out, "Wanna go blackberry picking, Cousin Hershel?"

He waves me away.

Margo comes out wearing Mama's gardening jeans, a faded long-sleeved shirt, and a floppy straw hat. Hershel snorts and says, "Margo, you going to a fashion show?"

"I'm not dignifying that with an answer," Margo says under her breath. To me she says, "Let's just find some berries and get back as fast as we can."

"Where's Calvin?" I ask.

"Who knows? I can't wait all day."

Margo's in such an all-fired hurry, I wear the shorts and T-shirt I have on. Calvin and Bo catch up to us at the barn. J.B. is at the blackberry thicket, "grazing" again. Josie is lying beside the far fence. She raises her head and watches us.

"Calvin, why don't you take that cow to the barn?" Margo asks. "I'll be a nervous wreck with her out here in the open."

"She's not thrilled to see you, either," Calvin says. "If you don't bother her, she won't bother you."

I run ahead and get to J.B. first. "I'm sorry, J.B." I point in Margo's direction. "I couldn't help it."

He looks around, flinches, and goes back to eating berries. When Margo walks up, he turns to look at her and busts out laughing. "Now ain't you a sight for sore eyes?"

Margo flashes him a smile. "I dressed up just for you, J.B. Any good berries left?" She hands me a bucket, gets one for herself, and holds one out to Calvin.

"I said I'd come with you," Calvin says. "I didn't say I'd pick berries." He heads for the creek. "I'm gonna check my minnows." Bo trots off behind him.

"You get back here, Calvin!" Margo yells in her bossy voice. "This'll take all day if you don't help!" She glances at J.B. and changes to a sweet sound. "That boy! Worrying with minnows while Mama's waiting for blackberries." She flutters her eyelashes. "How in the world can I get these berries picked without help?"

J.B. studies her, squares his shoulders, and says, "You'll manage, Margo." He turns sharp, like a marching soldier, and walks toward Polly.

I snicker, then say, "I'm here to pick, in case you didn't notice."

"Brat!" Margo starts picking berries fast and furious. When she puts her mind to it, she can pick almost as fast as

Mama. She wipes her forehead with her sleeve. "It's hotter than blazes out here."

The heat isn't what's bothering me. I'm wishing J.B. had stayed. But Margo's flirting and fussing drove him off and ruined everything. Except the berries. They're even bigger and juicier than when me and Mama picked. My first bucket fills up fast. On my way to get another bucket, I catch a June bug and set it to slow-motion crawling on the back of my hand.

"Jill! Put that nasty thing down!" Margo says. She makes a face and mutters, "What I wouldn't give for somebody to talk to."

"I'm here."

"Get back to picking," Margo says.

I hug my bucket between my arm and stomach so I can keep the June bug cupped in my hand. While I pick, I inch closer to Margo. The pinging of my berries mixes with the thunks coming from her half-full second bucket.

"There's a leaf in your hair," I say. I set my bucket on the ground. "Let me get it out for you." I reach up to lift her hat, set my June bug on her hair, put the hat back, and move to the other end of the blackberry patch.

Margo's hair is so thick, it takes a minute for her to notice the crawling. She lets out a little question-mark squeak, sets her blackberries down, takes off her hat, and feels around on her head. The June bug latches on to her finger. Margo screams and screams, flailing her hand around till she finally flings the June bug off. Still screaming, she turns to me.

I'm ready to run. But instead of coming at me, Margo gets big-eyed and takes off in the other direction. "Run, Jill!" she calls over her shoulder.

I turn to see Josie headed my way at a trot, her head lowered. There's no time to get away. I scuttle under the blackberry bushes, shielding my eyes from briars that rip my shirt, legs, and arms.

Josie veers away from the thicket, stops, and looks around. Margo is halfway between the blackberries and the pontoon, standing in one place and making little running motions as she stares at Josie. Her hands are over her mouth, like she's trying to stop her own squealing. Josie lifts her hoofs high and trots toward Margo.

"Over here, Margo! Hurry!" J.B. calls from Polly's deck.

"The pontoon, Margo!" I yell. "Get to the pontoon!" I crawl out and around the back edge of the thicket, yelling, "Run, Margo!"

Margo's feet finally move forward instead of up and down. She heads for the pontoon. Josie is gaining on her. Calvin runs up from the creek. He points at Josie and hollers, "Bo!" Bo lights out, barking and nipping at Josie's heels. She turns to butt and kick at him, then starts after Margo again. Bo's barking just gets Josie more riled up.

From the other direction I get to the pontoon the same time as Margo.

"Jump!" J.B. hollers. Margo flings herself up. With one hand she grabs Polly's rail. J.B. tugs on her arm. I latch on to her legs and boost her up. She's just cleared the railing when something hits me full force. I rocket sideways onto the ground as Josie whams into the pontoon's side, so close I feel a wave of hotness that's coming off of her.

It was Calvin, not Josie, that bowled me over. We're in a pile with him on top. He scrambles to his feet. "Come on!" he yells. The wind's knocked out of me so bad, I don't budge. Calvin grabs my hand and half drags me around to Polly's far side.

Josie keeps butting the pontoon. Every time she hits Polly, there's this wood-splintering noise.

Once I get my breath, me and Calvin climb up the weedy back side of the pontoon. J.B.'s chair is out on deck with Margo huddled in it, trembling and whimpering.

"You deserve a medal, Calvin!" J.B. pounds Calvin's shoulder. "Yessir. That was one high-powered tackle you saved Jill with." He winks at me. "And in the nick of time! She's little enough without Josie smushing her flatter'n a flitter."

Josie has quit butting the pontoon and is standing spraddle-legged, looking dazed. She lets out a long half moo, half groan.

"Way to go, Margo!" says Calvin. He climbs down and walks real slow toward Josie. "Upsetting our one and only cow. She'll likely give sour milk tonight." He's poised, ready to run if need be, as he rubs his hand down Josie's neck. She lows and swings her head toward him, more like she's asking "What happened?" than saying "I'm gonna chase you."

J.B. leans over the rail and asks, "Is she okay?"

"I think so," Calvin says. "She's got a real hard head. I'll put her in the holding pen to keep her calm."

We watch as Calvin and Josie and Bo amble off together toward the barn. J.B. chuckles and rubs his hand over his hair. "On her good days," he says, "there ain't a sweeter cow on God's green earth."

"Well, I've never seen one of her good days," Margo says. She turns on me. "This is all your fault!"

"I'm sorry, Margo." I look down, away from her. My

arms and legs are pockmarked with briars. I sit with my back against Polly's cabin and pull a few out. Where the big ones were, the holes bubble up with slow, thick blood.

"How do I get out of here?" Margo asks.

J.B. holds his hand up toward her like he's stopping traffic. "Before you leave, Margo, we need to have us a conversation"—he turns and looks at me—"about things a slip of a girl has no business hearing."

I sit up straight. "You can talk about anything in front of me, J.B."

He stares at me. "I believe I can." He looks up into the summer-sad tree leaves, then sits cross-legged on the deck next to Margo's chair, sideways to me. "Margo," he says, "the war and the prison camp and the hospitals and the hooch." He's talking where I can hear him plain. "They've all took their toll on me. I let 'em, mostly." He gives a little laugh. "It's the war took the fight out of me."

His voice gets this bitter taste. "But long as there's a breath in me, I ain't gonna sink low enough to ..." His eyes get watery. I pick at the briars in my legs so as not to notice, but Margo's sitting at attention, her hands clasped in her lap, looking straight at him.

"I got one pridesome thing left." He reaches over and pats Margo's hands real gentle. "From the day I laid my gun down, I never hurt nobody but me."

"You hurt my daddy." It comes out before I know it. I want to kick myself all around the deck. "I didn't mean that," I lie.

"Sure you did," J.B. says. "And it's the gospel truth." He frowns. "But that's a different hurt from what I'm talking now." He stands and looks down at Margo. "If there's one more drinking spell in me, and you was to sashay back here with me on my way to falling-down drunk …"

I snicker. "She'd be pretty mad, I can tell you!" I grin at Margo, but she's locked into what J.B.'s saying. Her face is paler than if Josie was hot on her heels.

"Jill, it's not her being *mad* that scares me. It's …" He looks at Margo. His voice softens so, I can barely hear. "Margo, that hooch? When it gets hold of a person, all them built-in cautions they was born with close down and …" He pauses like he's studying his next words. His face lights up. "Why, they get as unlike their real selves as a skunk without its scent—like Rabies."

With me right there and hearing every word, Margo and J.B. are looking at each other like they've shared a secret I'm not in on.

I spot Calvin on his way back from the barn. "Here comes Calvin!" I say, louder than I meant to. "Margo, Calvin'll help you get to the house."

J.B. waves at Calvin and walks toward Polly's cabin. "I got some iodine you can put on them scratches, Jill," he says.

"How about rubbing alcohol?" I ask. "Mama will see the iodine and wonder where I got it."

"Oh, J.B.!" Margo says. He stops and turns toward her. "You don't need to worry. I won't be coming back here alone."

He nods and goes into the cabin. Margo walks over to Polly's railing. I follow to help her down. She studies the rails, then grabs the top bar the right way—wrists facing out—like she'd been to rail-climbing school. Graceful as a cat, she scoots over the railing and lowers herself to the ground.

"That was good!" I say before I catch myself. I squat

down and look at her through the rails. "If you're blaming me for the June bug and Josie," I say, "you might also thank me for helping rescue you."

I expect a smarty answer. Margo looks me in the eye and says, "Thanks, Jill." She heads for the blackberry thicket, sets our berry pails in a basket, and hands it to Calvin to carry.

It's been a while since I looked at the pasture from Polly's deck. I settle into J.B.'s chair, then remember our agreement and climb down to wait at the carving tree.

The cabin door slams. "Found it!" J.B. hollers. He looks around the deck. "Found the alcohol!"

I wave at him and call out, "I remembered our no-girls-on-deck rule!"

After J.B. climbs down and gives me the alcohol, I'm sorry he found it. Dabbing it on the briar holes makes them sting like crazy. "Margo's gonna need peace and quiet to get over this day," I tell J.B. "She may lock me out of my own room!" I'm half joking, but it might happen.

"Poor Jill," J.B. says. "A grumpy sister in your room, a bone-lazy cousin in the yard, a drying-out drunk and a cantankerous cow in the pasture. You got no place to call your own."

Mama's whistle for me sounds. She's up from her nap. Since Margo and Calvin took all the berry pails, I've got no excuse to still be back here.

"Gotta hurry!" I put the top on the alcohol bottle and hand it to J.B., jump up, and sprint toward the house. While I'm still in shouting distance of J.B., I turn. "I've got a place to call my own!" I call out. "A good one!"

He's whittling and doesn't look up. I'm not gonna yell it for the whole world to hear. But my good place is right there on that tree root. Listening to stories and watching J.B. whittle newness out of wood that, to me, looks used up and over with. Speaking my mind to somebody who'll not call me "dummy."

Mama's making pie crust. She takes one look at me and says, "Jill, how many times do I have to tell you to wear long sleeves and pants when you pick blackberries?" She shakes her head. "You look like you did somersaults in a briar patch."

It's not my job to gather the morning eggs, but today Mama sent me for them. She's busy cooking. Every time she's in charge of a church supper, it takes up the better part of her week. Margo helps by shopping and chauffeuring and serving food the night of the supper.

I play with the kittens while I'm at the barn. By the time I get back to the house, the kitchen smells like spice cake. Mama is on the phone.

"Margo and I will drop him off after a while," she says. "One more thing, Cora. Tomorrow, can Josh stay overnight?" She listens, then says, "Good." She hangs up and mutters, "Thank the Lord for small favors."

I run water in the sink to rinse off the eggs. "Mama, I thought Daddy didn't want Cora keeping Josh while Hershel's here," I remind her.

Mama opens the oven. It's full to the brim with square cake pans. "I've got that church supper," she says. "Somebody's got to keep Josh between now and then. Are you volunteering, Jill?"

"No, ma'am."

Mama tests the front cake with a toothpick, takes the pan out, and sets it on the counter to cool. "Well, anyone who wants to watch Josh—and that includes Cliff—can call and tell Cora I've changed my mind."

Calvin comes in while Mama is turning the cakes out of their pans. He pretends to pinch a plug out of one; Mama swats his hand. He grins and gets out the peanut butter and jelly.

The steps are creaking. Hershel is on his way downstairs. The whole time he's been here, he's never gotten up in time to eat breakfast with the rest of us.

"Mama," I say, real serious. "Reckon Cora would keep Hershel, too?"

Mama chuckles. "Guess I'll leave him with you and Calvin, Jill."

"Hear that, Calvin?" I say low. "We're in charge of Cousin Hershel." Calvin is too busy licking the peanut butter knife to answer.

Hershel wanders into the kitchen. "My, Helen!" He sniffs loud and long. "That sure smells good. Don't recall ever having spice cake for breakfast before."

"Well, it's not happening today either, Cousin." Mama plops the last cake out of its pan. "These are for a church supper. There's not a crumb to spare."

"Oh." Hershel looks kind of pitiful. "Then what *is* for breakfast?"

"We had pancakes and sausage," I tell him. "With blueberries. Mama stirred them right into the batter."

Hershel sits at his usual place. "Sounds delicious."

"It was." I rub my stomach. "There's none left, though."

"Pancakes are better cooked fresh, anyway," Hershel says, reaching for his napkin.

Mama says nothing, just tears the cardboard strip off our new box of plastic wrap.

"A good night's sleep sure leaves a body hungry," Hershel says. It's like his words fall on the table in front of him and just lie there.

Margo comes through with a shopping bag full of Josh's stuff to carry to Cora's. She says, "Mama, we'd better put those cakes in the trunk, so Josh won't stick his foot in one."

Mama nods. "Calvin, help us load up."

"Can I help?" I ask. Mama never lets me carry food.

"You can get Cousin Hershel a cereal bowl," Mama says.

"I meant with the cakes." I plunk a bowl and spoon down in front of Hershel.

He mumbles, "I thought I'd get pancakes for breakfast. Blueberry pancakes." He looks like his last friend died.

I help load canned goods and utensils for the trip to church. As each thing is put in the car, Mama checks it off a list. Then she gets in and Margo starts the motor.

"You forgot something!" I yell. I run into the house and come back with Josh. Mama and Margo see what they left, and bust out laughing. I kerplunk Josh in Mama's lap. She musses his hair and says, "I should've had you on my list!"

As the car eases away, Mama rolls down her window. "Jill?" she calls. "If Cousin Hershel gets hungry, make him a couple of ham sandwiches."

Our grass is about dried up from lack of rain, but Calvin has the lawn mower out, cranking it up anyway. It starts and he heads for the side yard, where he always begins cutting our grass.

In the kitchen, Hershel is exactly how we left him. He asks, "Where's the cereal, Jill?" If his voice was smaller, he could double for Josh.

I open the cabinet door and point. "Take your pick, Cousin Hershel."

I flounce out to my room, which I'll have all to myself today, and get out a new jigsaw puzzle. But sunshine is streaming in my window so bright, I'd rather visit J.B. in the pasture.

On the kitchen table, the cereal box and milk pitcher are still next to Hershel's elbow. I decide to do one nice thing for him. I reach to put the milk back in the refrigerator. Hershel waves me away and shakes his head no. Through a mouthful of cornflakes, he says, "Gonna have seconds."

"Cousin Hershel," I say real sweet, "Mama said if she's not back by lunchtime, fix yourself a ham sandwich."

J.B. is at his usual whittling spot under our tree. He barely smiles when I say hi. I tell him about Josh almost getting left, and Hershel wanting pancakes. He brushes shavings off his pants and puts the carving he was working on in his pocket. I settle back for a story.

"Jill," he says, "I been thinking."

"What you thinking about, J.B.?"

"About all that's going on at your house. And about what a good long dried-out spell I've had since I moved onto this here pontoon." He leans both elbows on his knees and digs with his knife at grass between his feet. He cuts his eyes around at me. "Keep a secret?"

"Yeah." I cross my heart.

He picks up the clump of grass he's uprooted. "I'm going away."

"Huh?"

"It's time for me to leave."

"Oh, don't go, J.B.!" I beg. "With Hershel here, every

time we have fried chicken I can sneak you a drumstick. Maybe two."

"It ain't that, Jill." He faces me. There's this spark in his eyes. "My pontoon days, they've done their job. I'm ready to hope."

I think fast. "I can bring you a Sears catalog."

He shakes his head and laughs.

Something dawns on me. "It's Margo's fault! You're afraid she'll show up back here when you're drunk and helpless like Rabies without his scent." I stand and double up my fists. "I'll keep Margo away. If it comes to it, I can likely beat her up."

"Ain't nobody's 'fault,' Jill. Me wanting to leave is a good thing. A needful thing." He looks over at me. "If I'm ever gonna try, I ought to be about it."

J.B. stands up, fumbles in his pocket, and pulls out two carvings. One is Rabies. The other is the finished Bo.

"After I leave, will you give these to Margo and Calvin?" He runs his thumb over the carving of Bo and hands them both to me. "Yours is coming along, Jill. But it ain't finished."

I barely look at the carvings before stuffing them into my shorts pockets. No carving for me. Probably never will be. I'm the one he told his secret to. The one who, if he'd stay, would sneak him drumsticks. The one who'll miss him most.

J.B. puts his hand easy on my shoulder. His eyes are watery, like when he talked to Margo on deck. My eyes get watery, too. He pats me on the head and takes off at a lope toward the pontoon.

I tag after him. "Who's gonna keep you dried out, J.B.?"

He climbs aboard Polly. I holler up there, "Can't

nobody but Calvin keep you dried out."

"We'll see about that." He's all blurry, looking down at me. "Don't tell Calvin, okay? You crossed your heart."

Before I know it, I'm halfway up the side of the pontoon. J.B. says, "We got us a no-girls rule, remember?" He puts his rough hand over mine on the railing. "I likely won't leave today, Jill. But I wasn't gonna just vanish into thin air without a word to you." He turns and heads for the cabin. "Now, get outta here before we both start bawling!"

I carry the carving of Bo to last year's cave and set it on Calvin's arrowhead shelf. Where he'll never think to look. The skunk goes back in my pocket. It's mine. For now, at least.

At the barn, the gray kitten is sprawled on the feed room step, soaking up the sun. I scoop him up and set there, petting him till he settles in my lap. The lonesome feel of no J.B. at the pontoon pours over me like standing under a waterfall of sadness.

I try to imagine how it would be if things weren't so backwards. If Hershel was the fun one who carved and told stories, and if J.B. was the one we wish would go away.

I say it to Barney's kitten: "There's this dried-out drunk—J.B.'s his name—in that pontoon in the pasture. He's eating us out of house and home. We wait on him hand and foot. He's packing his bags. Good riddance, I say."

The story sounds like what it is, a bald-faced lie. The kitten flicks his ear where a tear fell on it and jumps out of my lap. I wipe my face with my shirttail and head for the house.

Calvin sees me coming, cuts the mower off, and meets

me on the path. "I have a plan, Jill," he says. "A plan that'll get rid of Hershel." Motioning for me to follow him, he hustles back toward where he was mowing, talking fast and low. "Firecrackers. We can scare him off with firecrackers."

"Whaaat?" I say it too loud. Calvin shushes me and looks toward Hershel in his chair.

"I'll shoot 'em off one at a time in the Howells' pasture." He pretends to show me something in a bed of Mama's flowers. "You tell Hershel the neighbors are shooting at Bo because he chases their cat. Tell him there's no telling who they'll hit."

I keep listening, but he quits talking. "That's it?" I finally say. "Can't Hershel tell a firecracker from a gun?"

"Not likely. Old Retread's a city slicker." Calvin stoops down and pulls a weed. "He'll be so scared of getting shot, he'll pack up and leave."

To my way of thinking, this is the worst plan Calvin has ever had. But I don't dare say so. I pull a weed and show it to Calvin. He nods.

"Well?" he asks.

"It might work." I try to sound like I believe myself.

"You got a better idea?" he snarls. "Once this church supper's over, we're liable not to have another chance."

I put my mind to it, but my head is so full of J.B. leaving, the firecrackers get all scrambled up with him. My better plan comes to me so fast, I spill it out to Calvin while I'm still thinking it through.

"How about this, Calvin? How about if you give J.B. some of the firecrackers? And ever' time you shoot one off in the Howells' pasture, he lights one up at the pontoon? That ought to sound like people shooting at other people, instead of at a dog. Wouldn't that be scarier?"

"Yeaaah," Calvin says slow and thoughtful. "You may have something there, Jill-girl." He bends down to pull another weed. Our car turns in at the driveway. Mama and Margo are back.

"Calvin, you better hurry to tell J.B. before ..." I almost blab J.B.'s secret.

"You tell him," Calvin says. "I'll get my firecrackers."

I head for the pasture. Now that we need J.B.'s help with something, maybe he'll stay.

J.B. isn't at the blackberry patch or the carving tree. I holler up to Polly's cabin but get no answer. There's not a sign of him along the creek bank.

I climb up Polly's side. Her deck is clean as a whistle. In the cabin, nothing's left but Calvin's sleeping bag, rolled up in a corner, and the other stuff we put there. I open every cabinet. "Don't be gone!" I say into the cabin's emptiness.

J.B.'s pretty much erased himself. The last place I check is the lift-up seat. The army helmet is in there. I sit cross-legged on the floor and hold it in my lap, like it's a warm, purring kitten.

Somehow, I took J.B.'s "likely won't leave today" as a promise instead of a probably. I wish I had put into words to him about my good place being our carving tree.

It takes a while for the gulping that hurts my stomach to change to little whimpers. I put the helmet back and go to the creek to wash my face.

"Jill? Jiii-ill!" Calvin calls. It sounds like he's halfway back here, and in a hurry. I hustle up the creek bank and flag him down. Bo has his nose to the ground, following a rabbit trail. Calvin takes one look at my face and asks, "What happened?"

"J.B." The tears get a fresh start. "He's gone."

Calvin about trips over his own feet running to the pontoon. He climbs up quick and down quicker. "Why'd he leave without saying a word to us?" he wonders out loud. He looks at me in a way that makes me squirm.

"He was gone when I got here," I say. It's the truth.

"You knew," Calvin says. It's not a question, so I don't answer.

Calvin turns and trots to the creek log. I'm right behind him. He looks inside the hollow tree. "He's not gone for good!" Calvin says, grinning and holding up a half-full bottle of whiskey. Bo plops down at our feet and sighs. Calvin puts the bottle back and says, "Mama sent me looking for you. We'd better get to the house."

On the path, Calvin says, "Margo's about to go to the grocery for Mama. I'll go with her and get more firecrackers. We're gonna need lots of firecrackers. And now that J.B.'s gone, Margo will have to help us get rid of Old Retread."

Fur and Fireworks

MAMA IS WORRIED ABOUT GRAY CLOUDS THAT ARE ROLLING IN. "We need rain," she says, "but if mud splashes on the butter beans, they'll rot."

As soon as Margo and Calvin get back from town, Mama sends us—Margo included—to pick beans. Calvin motions for me to pick the row next to him. "I got a hamburger at Mel's," he says. "Guess who's washing dishes there?"

I catch my breath and try to squash the hope I'm hoping. But I have to ask. "Somebody that likes coffee and steak in a diner better than mayonnaise sandwiches on a pontoon boat?"

"J.B.," Calvin says, like I hadn't already guessed right. He gets a butter bean out of my bowl and holds it next to one of his. "Don't pick 'em so flat. They ought to have big bumps like mine." He throws my bean away and says in

Margo's direction, "That hole Josie butted in the pontoon will make a good place to stash the firecrackers. And I'm gonna clear dry grass off a place to shoot 'em."

Margo says, "It'll be late afternoon tomorrow before I can get away from helping Mama at church."

"Then that's when we'll do it," Calvin says. "Jill, as soon as Margo gets here tomorrow, you go to the pontoon." He checks one of my beans to be sure the bumps are big enough. "When I shoot my first firecracker at the Howells', that'll be your cue to shoot back."

"Okay," I say. "When do we practice?"

Calvin makes his jaw-dropping, I-can't-believe-you're-that-dumb face. "Yeah, Jill," he says. "Let's practice. How about in front of Hershel's chair, so he'll be sure and hear? While we're at it, we'll explain the whole plan to him."

Margo looks across her bean row at me. "Have you ever shot a firecracker, Jill?"

"Mama and Daddy won't let me. But I've watched Calvin and Luther. I know how."

Margo turns to Calvin. "You put that cow up and I'll shoot the firecrackers. Let Jill deal with Hershel. She's a better liar than I am."

I hold my teeth together to keep from mentioning how many lies Margo told when she was getting Rabies de-scented.

"Once you light a firecracker, you gotta run," Calvin tells her. "Jill runs faster than you."

"I can run as fast as I want to," Margo says. "So that settles it. I'll do the firecrackers."

I'm still not convinced this plan of Calvin's will work. I know Hershel is lazy. But a lot depends on him being dumb, too. All morning I've practiced the lies I'm gonna tell him.

I hear a car in the driveway and run out to be sure it's Margo. She's getting out, balancing a piece of spice cake that's got Mama's caramel sauce drizzled over it. "Look what I brought you!" she calls over to Hershel. He follows her and that cake to the kitchen like a hungry puppy. The minute he's settled at the table, Margo and Calvin leave for the pasture.

I'm nervous about having to tell Hershel about the Howells. I try to make conversation. "The clouds are getting thicker and blacker," I say.

"Mmmmph." Hershel's mouth is full.

"I sure hope the rain holds off till people get to church to eat Mama's supper."

Hershel wipes the crumbs off his lips and mutters, "Don't see why she's across town cooking for other people while I'm left here with sandwiches"—he looks at me— "and a houseful of useless children who won't even hand a body a box of cereal." He heads out to his lawn chair.

I hope with all my might that the rain holds off till we've scared Hershel. I can't wait to watch a taxi pull out of our driveway loaded down with him and his appetite and his after-shave lotion and his lawn chair.

The first firecracker pops in the Howells' pasture. I check in the mirror to be sure I look worried, then poke my head out the back door. A firecracker bangs in our pasture.

"What's that?" I call to Hershel.

He yawns. "Sounds like firecrackers."

A "shot" sounds in the Howells' pasture. "That's not firecrackers!" I holler. Another firecracker goes off in our pasture. "That's gunfire!"

Calvin answers Margo with three "pops."

"You better get in here, Cousin Hershel!" I hold the screen wide open. "The Howells are shooting at Bo for chasing their cat! You're liable to get hit any minute!"

Bo starts howling in the garage. I'm telling the wrong lie. I say fast, "I mean, the Howells must be shooting at the Vinsons."

"Don't worry." Hershel flits his hand toward me. "It's firecrackers."

Margo fires off a volley. She must've lit a whole string.

Hershel waits for the noise to die down and says, "I know firecrackers when I hear them. My despicable neighbors shoot them year-round." He raises his eyebrows. "Evidently, so do yours."

Bo is howling so loud, I run outside to holler, "You better come in the house, Hershel! That's the Howells and the Vinsons, shooting up this whole end of the country!" I don't have to fake being desperate. If Calvin finds out I got my stories mixed up, I might as well move.

Hershel picks up a magazine and leans back in his chair. "I'd rather be out here with firecrackers than in a living room full of beans," he says.

Our pasture suddenly sounds like the grand finale at a Fourth of July celebration. Calm as he's acting, Hershel still flinches.

Calvin doesn't answer with a single firecracker. "Think I'll creep back and see if we've got any neighbors left," I tell Hershel.

"Be careful," he says like he doesn't mean it, and yawns.

Rabies is so frantic, I decide to take him with me. He claws my arms when I lift him out of the cage. Holding him runs a close second to jumping into blackberry bushes.

The air around Polly smells burnt. "It didn't work," I tell Margo. "Hershel knew it was firecrackers."

Calvin runs up to us, hollering, "What in the world, Margo?" His voice is uppy-down and crackly. "You want Hershel to believe our neighbors own machine guns?"

"Don't fuss at me!" Margo comes back at him. "I got nervous. If you wanted them shot one at a time, you should've untangled them."

"What I should've done," he says, "is let Jill do the shooting." He crams his almost-full sack of firecrackers under the pontoon and lopes off toward the house.

Margo takes Rabies out of my arms. "Poor baby. Let's go to the house, where we belong." She cuddles her skunk. "Bring those firecrackers, will you, Jill? The rest of mine are under there, too."

I stick my arm through the hole but can't reach the sacks. "My arm's not long enough!" I yell.

"Honestly!" Margo comes back, hands me Rabies, and reaches in for the firecrackers. "I can't believe I'm grappling around inside a boat's bottom!" She jerks the sacks out. As they fall to the ground, loose firecrackers dribble out into the grass and weeds.

Margo takes Rabies again. "My poor baby is so upset, I'm gonna let him stay in the house awhile."

"Not in my room!" I tell her. "Leave him in his carrying case in the living room."

"Hurry up!" is the only answer I get.

I squat down to pick up the firecrackers. In Calvin's sack I can feel some long, skinny boxes. I take a peek. The boxes are sparklers. Calvin used to get me sparklers whenever he bought fireworks. These are bound to be for me.

The grass around Polly is so dry, I take matches and a

box of sparklers to the creek. I light one. It blooms into a hissing white-light flower. Sparks fall into the water with little *ssfft* sounds. I take off my shoes, wade out with a lit sparkler, and twirl round and round. The fizzy sparks prickle where they land on my hand and arm. With the next sparkler I twirl in the opposite direction.

Once the box has nothing but burnt stems in it, I go back to Polly. There's other stuff in Calvin's sack. Cherry bombs and firecrackers bigger than the ones he and Margo made gun noises with. Another box of kitchen matches.

I untangle a big firecracker and hold it at arm's length, hold an unlit match to its fuse, whisper, "Sssssssssss ... *boom*!" The *boom* makes me jump.

I pretend-light the thing time and time again. Before I know it, my hand is striking the match and touching it to the fuse. A spark shimmies downward. I throw the firecracker away as hard as I can. It hits Polly and bounces to the ground close to my feet. I scuttle away; the explosion comes, louder than loud.

A puff of smoke hangs where the firecracker blew up. Below it, tiny strands of fire are spreading every which way like lines on a roadmap. One snakes toward the sacks. I need something that'll hold water.

I clamber up Polly's side and grab the army helmet out of its lift-up bench. Halfway to the creek, I look back just as Calvin's sack flares up, like its whole box of matches is on fire. There's a tiny quietness before firecrackers start exploding so fierce, it sounds like a world war has set up shop in our pasture.

Two bottle rockets whiz crazy up into the air. I drop the helmet and run for the house, past Josie bellowing in the holding pen toward Bo's howls coming from the garage.

Calvin meets me on the path, running hard. "I didn't mean to," I holler, and turn to follow him back toward the pasture. As we pass Josie, he yells, "Between you and Margo, everything on this place is scared silly except Hershel."

The firecracker racket dies down almost as quick as it started. Where the sacks were, two scorched circles are littered with paper hulls. A lonesome sparkler fizzes close to the pontoon. Ground fires flicker all over the place in the dry grass.

"Stay back!" Calvin says. "I'll bring the feed buckets." He sprints off toward the barn.

I grab the helmet from where I dropped it and run to the creek. Before it's good and full, Calvin comes clanging down the bank with two buckets.

"You fill 'em," he says. "I'll fight the fire."

The creek is so low, I have to lay the buckets on their sides. The world narrows down to water sliding across a tin rim, a suction slurp when Calvin yanks up each full bucket, the rustle of an empty one settling into creek gravel.

A splat on the tin bucket un-hypnotizes me. Heavy, far-apart raindrops are stirring tree leaves and smacking the creek water. Calvin trades an empty bucket for the full one. "We're gaining on it," he says.

The rain changes to thick and fast, beats a drum song on the bucket, and soaks me to the skin. My hair hangs in streams around my face.

Calvin has shed his shirt. His chest is shiny wet. "Keep filling 'em," he says.

Buckets come and go. The rain is ghost-white now, mixed with hot-air fog. Calvin shakes my elbow and tugs for me to stand up. I follow him up the bank.

What was once grass around the pontoon is a soggy black tangle. The lower half of Polly's side where the sacks were is black, too. Calvin stands spraddle-legged, his arms folded, looking at the mess, then at me. I brace myself for the bawling out I deserve.

"The fire's out," he says. "You were good help, Jill-girl." He picks up his shirt, wrings it out, and gets the feed buckets. "Go on to the house. I'll check on Josie."

The backyard looks washed clean. And empty. Hershel must've taken his precious chair indoors. Our car is gone, too. Margo is at church by now, helping serve the dinner.

After a bath, I wrap our biggest towel around me twice and drip my way toward my room. Calvin is just inside the back door, shedding soaked clothes. The carrying case, with Rabies asleep in it, is next to our butter bean mountain.

Margo's things aren't in my room. I dress fast and run up the steps. Her stuff is piled on her bed. There's not a trace of Hershel. I let out a whoop and slide down the steps on my bottom.

"Hershel's gone!" I yell. Rabies scrunches into a tighter ball. "We did it, Calvin!"

"Hallelujah!" he hollers from the bathroom. "My plan worked!" He comes out with a towel around his waist and gives me a big grin as he heads upstairs.

I'm so happy, I jump up and down all alone in the kitchen. Then a thought hits me. As soon as Calvin comes downstairs, I ask, "Is Mama gonna be mad?"

A car crunches the driveway gravel. "Guess we'll find out soon enough," he says.

Margo comes in carrying an armload of pans. "Hey, Margo!" Calvin says. "Old Retread has hit the road."

"I know," she says. "Didn't Jill tell you I've moved out of her pig sty?"

Mama and Daddy come in, their arms full of pots and pans. "Calvin, help us unload," Daddy says. "The girls can put this stuff where it belongs." The three of them go out to the car.

"I sure didn't think Calvin's plan would work," I tell Margo.

"It didn't!" she says. "Me bringing Rabies into the house is what got rid of Hershel."

"Rabies chased Cousin Hershel?" I giggle at the idea.

"No, dummy! I never took him out of his case." Margo climbs up in a chair to reach our highest shelf. "When Hershel saw Rabies, he said, 'I will not stay in the same house with a skunk!' I told him that my skunk was so upset, I was gonna let him spend the night in our house. Hershel said, 'If that skunk stays, I go!' He went straight upstairs and packed his bags."

I stare up at Margo. "You mean we didn't need to set the pasture on fire?"

Margo groans. "If I'd brought Rabies in a long time ago, Hershel would've knocked us down getting out the door."

Calvin comes clattering in with another load of pans. Margo whispers, "Don't tell Calvin."

I mouth, "I won't," and cross my heart.

"I told Mama about Hershel," Calvin says.

"Is she mad?" I ask.

He grins. "She said, 'Thank the Lord for big favors.'"

This afternoon has already lasted a month. Margo is at her friend Clare's, and Calvin is somewhere mowing. I'm keeping Josh out from under foot while Mama cans butter beans.

Usually Josh likes being outdoors. But today it's too hot. The air is sticky and hard to breathe. I try playing catch, Josh's favorite and worst thing. He misses a few times and sits down hard on the ground with his arms crossed and his lower lip stuck out.

Sometimes, hide-and-seek works. But Josh won't hide or seek. I drag him to the swing, where I've stashed some books. Halfway through the first one, he shoves the others onto the ground. "Brat!" I yell as I squat to pick up the books.

Josh scoots out of the swing, whines, "Wanna play with Rabies!" and runs back toward the pen.

I tear out after Josh. He's already at the pen and is fiddling with the latch.

If ever there was a day Josh hasn't earned time with Rabies, this is it. I jerk his arm away and say, "Young man, you're going inside this very minute!" and drag him toward the house. He howls and kicks and tries to pull away. Through the screen door I warn Mama, "I'm bringing Josh in. He's acting awful."

"You, Josh!" She's ladling raw beans into a huge pot of boiling water. "You settle down and behave yourself!" Under her breath she adds, "Jill, wash his face with a cold rag, and keep him occupied till I get these beans to blanching."

As we pass the stove, Mama moves so she's always between us and the hot water. "Seems to me," she calls after us, "little boys who mind their sisters ought to have ice cream before a nap."

Ice cream is a magic word. Josh settles down. By the

time Mama brings us bowls of vanilla with our names written in chocolate syrup, we've worked two of his puzzles and read a book.

Mama puts Josh down for his nap. I go to my room and settle across the bed on my stomach to read.

"Jill." The name comes from far off. I push it away.

"Jill. Wake up." Josh is right in my face. His breath smells like ice cream. Or a baby's breath. My book is beside me on the bed.

"Hep me, Jill."

I roll away from him. "Help you what, Josh?" I stretch my arms and legs as far as they'll go. I don't want to wake up.

"Find Rabies."

The sitting up and grabbing his shoulders is one motion. "What?"

He giggles real quiet, puts his finger to his mouth. "Shhh. Hide and seek."

I relax, feeling silly and asleep. "I thought you'd lost Rabies."

Josh takes my hand and tugs on it. "He's in the peaches." He pulls me toward the front door, which we almost never use. It's unlocked and open. We circle to the backyard. I run to Rabies' pen. I know before I look that the pen is empty. When Josh was supposed to be napping, he must've snuck out the front door and turned Rabies loose.

Josh is standing off a ways, looking blank. I kneel in front of him. It's all I can do not to shake him within an inch of his life. "Where's Margo's skunk?"

"Hiding." Josh points toward the orchard and starts

marching back there, his back stiff and straight with knowing what I don't.

I run ahead of Josh to the orchard. There's not a sign of a skunk anywhere.

"Okay, Josh." I get on my knees, hold his shoulders, and look him in the eye. "Where did you see Rabies last?"

He leads me over to the tangled fencerow between the orchard and the barnyard. "I hid him." He squats and points into weeds under the bushes. "There."

I crawl through stick-tights and briars, searching the whole fencerow. All around the orchard and barnyard we call, "Rabies! Here, Rabies!" I almost send Josh to the house for raisins, but then remember the boiling water and go myself. Josh stays at the orchard, calling Rabies in a snuffledy voice.

Quarts of butter beans are lined up on the counter. Mama is cleaning up the kitchen.

"Mama, Josh turned Rabies loose in the orchard. We can't find him." Without me even telling her what I came for, she grabs a box of raisins and some unshelled peanuts and beats me out the door.

Mama covers the same ground Josh and I have been over, and more. We make a trail of peanuts and raisins that leads to Rabies' pen. As soon as Calvin gets home from mowing, he searches the pasture. And comes back empty-handed. Mama gives him a cut-up apple to add to the skunk trail.

I'm too miserable to hope. I want to blame Josh, but I can't. He's little. If I hadn't fallen asleep, I would've heard him unlock the front door. Rabies would be safe in his cage.

Margo gets home after dark. She's all bubbly about

Clare's new wallpaper and about winning a challenge in band.

Calvin comes in from one last check of the orchard. I can tell by looking at him that he didn't find Rabies. I'm hoping we don't tell Margo until morning. Maybe the apple will lure him home.

"Calvin, let me borrow your flashlight," Margo says. "I ought to go tell Rabies good night."

I hold my breath. Calvin mumbles, "My batteries are about gone. Just wait till morning."

Margo yawns. "Oh, all right. I'm worn out anyway." She goes to the back door and yells through the screen, "Good night, Rabies! I love you!"

I expect Mama to speak up, but she keeps wiping the stove. Margo hugs her, says, "Night, all," and heads toward the stairs.

Mama waits for the fifth step to creak, then asks, "Any sign of Rabies?"

Calvin shakes his head no and puts up his flashlight.

In the early morning dimness, I sit up wide awake. I may have heard a stair barely squeak. I pull on yesterday's jeans and a long-sleeved shirt, pick up my shoes, and ease out of my room. Calvin is tiptoeing toward the back door.

When we're far enough away from the house to talk, we don't. The raisins and peanuts and apple are gone, but that doesn't mean much. We could leave a raw elephant out there and critters would eat it overnight.

I start searching at the hedges where Josh hid Rabies. Last night's spider webs are everywhere. Cold dew drenches the knees of my jeans. I'm pulling a big clump of grass apart to check in it when Calvin's feet appear outside the bush I'm under. "Jill. Come here."

I follow him to the barnyard. He points to little bits of black and white fur that lead into undergrowth. A good-sized piece of Rabies' tail is lying out in the open. There aren't any bones.

I pick up what's left of Rabies' tail and hug it to me. Crying starts hot in my chest and rises in big, hurting gulps. Calvin says, "I'll get a shovel."

I sit on a rock and part a line between the white and black fur, sing-songing "I'm sorry, Rabies. I'm so sorry. "

Calvin brings a little paper sack from the house. We put every scrap we can find of Rabies' fur in it. Then Calvin disappears toward the pasture. He comes back with the army helmet. "The coffin," he says.

We pick a shady spot at the edge of the orchard. While Calvin digs, I pad the helmet with dandelions and grass, wild rose petals and clover. On top of the padding I arrange Rabies' fur and tail, then cover them with a blanket of pale green moss.

When Calvin sees what I've done, he nods, gets down on his knees beside the grave, and takes the helmet. With one hand spread over the moss, he flips the helmet right side up, centers it in the hole he's dug, stands up, and reaches for the shovel.

"Shouldn't Margo be here?" I ask.

"No need for her to see how little's left."

I sit on the ground next to the grave, hugging my knees and crying again, counting shovelfuls. In no time Rabies is just a bare mound of dirt. Calvin packs the grave down with the back of his shovel, then piles rocks on it. I'm scrunched in a wad, staring at the rocks.

Calvin stands tall and looks down at me. "You're not to

blame, Jill." He squats on one knee. "Josh was supposed to be asleep."

"But he wasn't," I whimper. Somewhere beyond the sadness, I wonder if Calvin will hug me. He doesn't. But he rests his hand gentle on my shoulder.

"Mama needs to know," he says. "Let's go to the house."

If it was up to me, I'd say Rabies' mama found him and talked him into staying with her. I'd let Margo wander back to the orchard from now on, hoping to find her skunk even after he's full grown.

But Mama tells her. Margo starts bawling. "I didn't even go tell him good night," she moans.

"He wasn't there to tell, Margo," Calvin says. Mama gives him a hard look.

Margo wants a funeral, so we all go back to the grave. I get a head start, pick daisies along the way, and pretty up the grave rocks with them.

Mama says a little speech about what a nice skunk and good pet Rabies was. In her prayer, she gives thanks that Margo went ahead and had him de-scented "because, Lord, he's been a joy to us all. Amen."

Josh sniffles through the beginning of his favorite prayer, "God is great, God is good." Calvin jumps in with "Amen" before Josh gets to the "Let us thank him for this food" part. Margo boo-hoos through it all. Back at the house, she goes straight to her room.

I wander into the kitchen, wishing I had words or ways of comfort like some people do. Mama is making a pitcher of lemonade. Lemonade for Margo is like ice cream for Josh. Especially Mama's. She starts with hot water, so everything blends itself real nice.

Mama pours lemonade into Margo's favorite glass. She adds ice and a sprig of mint. "Jill," she says, "why don't you take this up to Margo?" On top of the ice cubes, she sets a maraschino cherry with its stem still attached.

"Me?" I look at her like she's got me mixed up with somebody else.

"Yes, you." She adds a straw and hands me the glass. "You'll know what to do."

Nobody's ever said that to me before. I take the lemonade. On my way upstairs, I stop by my room to get something that belongs to Margo.

I'm afraid if she knows it's me, Margo will tell me to go away. So as I tap on the door, I open it and go in without waiting to be invited. She's sitting in a straight chair at the window, staring out at a tree.

"Mama made you some lemonade."

"I don't want any lemonade." She reaches for a tissue and blows her nose. I set the glass on the window ledge. I'm afraid to say anything, so I just stand there. Margo looks like a statue. A statue staring out the window with eyes so full of stone tears, a blink'll send them rattling down its face.

Finally I say, "It wasn't Josh's fault. I shouldn't have gone to sleep."

"Mama didn't tell me much." She reaches for the glass and takes a sip. "What happened? I want to know."

I tell her. When I get to the part about Josh's nap, Calvin would be proud—I don't blame myself. What I say is that Josh is just a little boy who wanted to play. That he didn't mean any harm.

To the tree outside her window, Margo says, "I know that."

I'm real careful when I tell about Calvin finding Rabies. I don't want Margo to know that all we found was fur. Or that we used a helmet off a dead soldier for the coffin.

Margo takes the last sip of lemonade, sets the glass back on the ledge, stands up, and sobs, "I just loved Rabies so much ..." She turns and flings herself face down across the bed, her head cradled on her arm. Her whole self cries so hard, the bedsprings creak.

When the great sobs begin to calm, I sit down on the side of the bed, wondering if I ought to pat her.

A brush is on the bureau across the room. I get it, set J.B.'s carving of Rabies beside Margo's jewelry box, and ease myself up on the bed to where I can reach her hair. When I first start brushing, she stiffens. But she doesn't jerk away.

By the fortieth brush stroke, Margo's shoulders settle in and she's breathing steady. I quit counting at two hundred.

Every day I pick flowers for Rabies' grave so it doesn't look bare when Margo visits it. The daisies in the orchard are about used up. I guess I'll have to look in the pasture for some pretty ones. I don't go back there much since J.B. left. Even with the sun shining and birds singing, it feels lonesome and creepy.

J.B. is sitting in his regular spot under our tree, with Josie grazing nearby. Him being there looks so natural, at first I head that way at a regular walk. Then I take off running.

"Hey there, J.B.!" I holler. He looks up from carving, waves, and motions me to my root. I sit down and hug my knees to keep from hugging J.B.'s neck. "You're back!" I say, like he didn't know that.

"I been waiting for you," he says. "Came by yesterday, too."

"I'm not back here much anymore," I say. "How you been, J.B.?"

"I been okay, Jill. Maybe a mite better than okay." He flicks the knife blade toward Polly. "I haven't set no fires. Where'd your pontoon get that five o'clock shadow?"

Now that he mentions it, the scorched spots on Polly do make her look like she could use a shave. I laugh loud. "That's a good one, J.B.!"

All in a rush, I tell about the firecrackers, and about how rain and Calvin put out the fires, and how Hershel left on account of Rabies being in the house. And what happened to Rabies.

"Margo's tore up about it. All of us, for that matter. But at least Margo's got her room back." I glance quick at J.B. "Why, soon as you move back to the pontoon, every one of us will be where we fit best!"

J.B. gets this sad smile. "I ain't moving back to the pontoon, Jill. I told you that already." He folds the carving knife, puts it in his pocket, and looks me full in the face. "Remember, on the pontoon with Margo, how you said I could talk about anything in front of you?"

I nod.

"I'm doing good, Jill. With no half-pint girl and nearly growed boy watching over me, I been sober ever since I left." He leans back against the tree. "I been working at Mel's."

"Calvin told me."

"Been showing up regular. On time. Got me a schedule."

"You get much overtime?" I ask.

J.B. laughs. "Dishwashing's not exactly an overtime type

job. But them carvings of mine? Folks buy 'em quick as Mel puts 'em out. They pay better than the dishwashing."

He digs in his pocket, puts some bills on the ground between us, and weights them down with a carving that's been hid behind him. "The money's what I owe Calvin," he says.

I put the money in my pocket and pick up my carving. It's of our tree, with us—me and J.B.—under it. Him whittling and me watching. I study every line and leaf.

"It's perfect, J.B." I say.

He ducks his head. "That's not the only reason I came back, Jill. I wanted to tell you something that's been in the back of my mind for a good while now." He shuts his eyes. "Maybe, just *maybe*, I'm ready to start me a good new life."

I want to remind him how much he claimed to like his old pontoon life. But he opens his eyes and keeps talking. "I been steering clear of that hollow tree for a good while now." He stares off into space. "I got me a hope ... about a little place of my own with a shelf in plain sight. A job—maybe washing dishes—that'll keep food on the table ..."

"Why does your hope have a shelf, J.B.?"

"To set that almost-empty bottle on." He grins at me. "I figure, if something's in arm's reach, it ain't as tempting."

"You been planning, like Calvin does," I tell him.

"That's not the half of it, Jill! Here's the best part—I'm going to Idaho!"

"Idaho?" My voice goes up and down like Calvin's. "That's a whole world away from here."

"You got that right. I'm heading out tomorrow." J.B. chuckles. "To a world away from here. Idaho."

I watch Josie cropping grass. If I couldn't talk J.B. out of leaving the pontoon, there's not a chance I can convince him to not go to Idaho. All I can think to say is, "Tomorrow?"

"Got my duffel bag packed," he says. "I was waiting for a chance to tell you."

"You got a bottle in that duffel bag?"

"Yep. The about-empty one from the hollow tree."

I rub my finger along the tree trunk in my carving and say what my mind knows is wasted breath. "Don't go, J.B."

His eyes get watery. "It's good to know somebody's gonna miss me." He blinks his eyes clear and looks at me. "But I'm going."

My fingers wander along the knife strokes in my carving. It's like the wood is slipping me words to say. "J.B. It seems to me ..." I work at keeping my voice from shaking. "Somebody who whittled this out of throwaway wood"— I hold up my carving—"can carve himself a pretty good life in Idaho."

J.B. stands tall and salutes me. "Young'un, that there is the very handle this soldier needed for holding on to his hope!" He does a soldier about-face and marches off. I try to stay still. But before I know it, I'm tagging along.

"You gonna write or call, J.B.?" I ask.

He says, "Halt, two, three," and steps out of being a soldier. He gives me a quick hug and a small smile. "This is goodbye, Jill." He points behind me. "Go have yourself a mighty fine life."

J.B. walks away. He doesn't look back, but I wave until he disappears beyond the far hill. Then I go sit at our tree, waiting for the tightness in my throat to ease up. Letting it sink in that, this time, J.B. is gone for sure.

I count Calvin's money. By my calculations, it's more

than he's had at once in his nearly fourteen years. Since I'm carrying it to him, he ought to buy me something. Maybe more sparklers.

On my way to the house, one of Barney's kittens—the gray one—tries to follow me. At first, I shoo him back toward the barn. On second thought, I scoop him up.

He's not black and white. But he's awful cute. Maybe Margo will take a liking to him.